Dear Readers,

This month, celebrate Mother's Day with the best kind of treat: four new love stories from Bouquet. Then again, *any* day is the right day to read romance. . . .

Marcia Evanick, veteran Silhouette and Loveswept author, starts off this month with the first in the three-book Wild Rose series, **Wife In Name Only,** in which a marriage undertaken for the sake of the children becomes a surprisingly passionate union. Next up, the talented Jacquie D'Alessandro offers **Kiss the Cook,** the charming tale of a determined caterer—and the sexy financial whiz who tempts her to turn up the heat in her kitchen.

Adam's Kiss, from another promising new author, Patricia Ellis, takes us to a Wisconsin farm, where a dispute between neighbors becomes a kiss across the fence . . . and maybe much more. Tracy Cozzens wraps up the month with her latest book for Zebra, **Seducing Alicia,** the suspenseful story of a scientist who finds herself falling for an unexpected man—without any idea that her new beau may not be exactly what he seems.

Feel the thrill of tenderness and tears, desire and delight. And when you sit back with the four breathtaking Bouquet romances this month, remember to enjoy!

Kate Duffy
Editorial Director

ADAM'S KISS

"Everything all right?"

Amelia nodded. "Sure, why wouldn't everything be all right?"

He walked a few steps closer, which brought him next to her chair. Adam crossed his arms over his solid chest and shrugged. "I don't know. Maybe because you didn't get up to answer the door and because you haven't moved an inch since I walked in."

Thinking fast under pressure had never been a strong suit of Amelia's. "Well, I'm sorry I didn't get to the door, but I think I fell asleep sitting here watching television and then you caught me off guard."

"Uh-huh."

He didn't look as if he believed her. In fact, instead of being a gentleman and at least pretending he believed her, he leaned forward and rested his hands on the arms of the chair, crowding her with his presence, with his scent and his sexy blue eyes.

"Wha—what are you doing?"

"Nothing," he said softly. "Why? Are you uncomfortable?"

She tried to avoid his gaze but couldn't. "I'm not uncomfortable. Why would you think that?"

"You know, I've spent my life doing a lot of physical . . . labor."

And he had the body to show for it, she thought. Her focus then shifted to his lips and she couldn't help but think that no one should be allowed to be this sexy and this close to her without—

His lips settled on hers in midthought and Amelia sighed. His kiss was firm and confident and coaxing and demanding. Perfect. Lips that sexy just had to be this good at kissing.

ADAM'S KISS

PATRICIA ELLIS

Zebra Books
Kensington Publishing Corp.

http://www.zebrabooks.com

For Kirk, for making the romance I dreamed about reality.

ZEBRA BOOKS are published by

Kensington Publishing Corp.
850 Third Avenue
New York, NY 10022

Zebra and the Z logo Reg. U.S. Pat. & TM Off.

First Printing: May, 2000
10 9 8 7 6 5 4 3 2 1

Printed in the United States of America

ONE

Amelia steered the old white van along the county road, her eyes searching for the white rail fence gate and red mailbox that she remembered marked the entrance to her Aunt Gracie's property. She sighed. "My property now, I guess. Right, guys?"

She looked over at the passenger seat and smiled. Junior, her three-year-old shepherd/lab mix woofed happily from his copilot's seat. From the back of the van, various other animal sounds joined Junior. "What do you think, girls?" she asked the three sisters in separate cat carriers. Olga, Masha, and Irina meowed unhappily. "Don't worry. I'll let you out in a few minutes. We're almost there. I think."

Amelia peered again at the passing scenery. It looked familiar, but not that familiar. "I might have to stop and ask directions."

A pitiful whine emanated from a small carrier on the floor. Amelia reached back between the two front seats and stuck her fingers through the grate in the front of the carrier. A tiny tongue licked her fingers. "Aw, Fife, don't worry. Once we get to the farm, everything will be all right." The Chihuahua puppy yipped, a barely audible sound, and Amelia returned her concentration to the road ahead of her.

A gate came into sight up ahead and Amelia slowed. There was a large mailbox with the name Larsen emblazoned on the side in white block letters. "Why does that name seem familiar?" she asked Junior. "Maybe Aunt Gracie mentioned it." She shrugged and asked, "What do you think, guys? Should we stop in and ask the Larsens where the Appleberry place is or should we drive on and hope that we find it on our own?"

A series of barks, meows, and yips didn't offer much advice. "All right, we'll ask for help," she said after a moment. But before she could turn onto the road that led to the Larsen property, a truck rumbled toward her and began turning onto the road. It slowed when she hopped out of the van and waved.

The driver stopped the truck and opened his door, his booted feet hitting the gravel drive evenly. Amelia started toward him. He wore jeans and a cotton shirt with a baseball cap on his head sporting the logo of a tractor manufacturer.

Amelia shaded her eyes in the bright summer sunshine. He seemed to be of average height and build, but moved with a sense of confidence that Amelia envied for a moment before she spoke.

"Hello. I wonder if you could help me out. I'm looking for the Appleberry place."

He halted his approach about fifteen feet away and Amelia saw him look from her to her van and back. "Sure," he finally said. "It's about a mile or so farther down this road on the left."

His voice was surprisingly rich and resonant. Sexy,

Amelia thought. Then she shook a mental finger at herself and smiled at the man. "Thanks. I thought I was getting close, but had begun to doubt myself."

He took a few more steps toward her and Amelia found herself looking up into his clear blue eyes. Strands of thick golden brown hair showed from underneath the cap and his tanned skin bespoke time spent working outside. "Are you the niece?"

His abrupt question took Amelia by surprise. She nodded. "Yes. I'm Amelia Appleberry. My Aunt Grace left me the property when she passed away recently."

He nodded, his eyes moving over her face with a strange intensity that made her breath catch in her throat. "My name is Adam Larsen. I was your aunt's neighbor."

Amelia nodded, wondering why it seemed that he expected her to know his name. Then it hit her. Larsen. "Oh, I remember now. You're the man who wanted to buy the property. I'm sorry, Mr. Larsen," she smiled happily, contemplating a peaceful existence on her own small Wisconsin farm, "but right now I'm not interested in selling."

He just nodded. "You plan on living there?"

"Yes, I do. Until I figure out what I want to do."

Adam's brow wrinkled as he frowned in confusion. "Do what?"

"That's just it," Amelia confessed, not sure why she felt so at ease with this stranger. "I don't know what I want to do. But now that I have a place to live and enough money to see me through a few months at the least, maybe I can figure it out."

He didn't say anything, but continued to look at her oddly. Amelia wondered if she'd said too much. She usually did. "Well, I have to get going, Mr. Larsen—"

"Adam," he said abruptly.

"Adam," she repeated, liking the sound of his name. "I have to get us all settled in at my aunt's place before dark."

"Us?"

She waved at the van as she walked toward it. "Just my menagerie. I have a few animals. And I guess I've inherited a few more. A Mr. Winslow is supposed to be taking care of them until I get there."

"I'm sure everything's fine," he assured her.

Amelia pulled open the door to the van and climbed in, Adam Larsen following her slowly to the door. "I'm glad to hear that," she said. "I love animals and I was a little worried about them since no one was really in charge here."

Adam rested his large, callused hands on the door of the van and regarded her silently. Then Amelia saw his gaze shift to Junior, who sat in the passenger seat, his harness holding him in place.

"You have a seat belt for your dog?"

Amelia smiled. "Of course. What would happen if I had to stop quickly?"

He just nodded. "Makes sense. I guess."

"Of course it does. Thanks again for the directions, Adam. I'll try to be a good neighbor."

She waved as she started the van and put it in gear. He stepped back and raised a hand in a sort of wave as she rolled on down the road. Amelia stole a glance at him through her sideview mirror and grinned. "Well, guys, things are looking up. We have a cute next door neighbor who seems nice. Quiet, but nice. He's probably married with about six kids, but you can't have everything, now, can you?"

Junior barked happily while the three sisters yowled their displeasure at still being cooped up. Fife quivered, then suddenly growled as menacingly as his tiny body could manage.

Amelia glanced down. "What is it, Fife? Oh, Zilla, what are you doing out? Leave Fife alone."

The iguana paid her no attention, continuing to peer through the metal grating at the tiny dog. Amelia scooped her up and put her on the dashboard in the sunshine. "There you'll feel better with a little sun to warm you up."

She slowed as she approached the end of the mile Adam had told her about. On her right was a large sign announcing Ned and Nan's Taxidermy and Cheese Emporium. Amelia blinked at the sign for a moment. "Okey-dokey. That's one place I have to visit. But don't worry, guys. I won't make any of you come along."

She looked back to the left and continued slowly. Then she saw it. The white fence gate with the red wooden mailbox. Appleberry was written on the mailbox in white paint. It looked very homemade. Amelia smiled. She was going to like it here.

"Thanks, Aunt Gracie," she whispered, and turned onto the drive that led to her new home.

Adam Larsen stomped into his house, the door banging shut behind him. What kind of wacky female made a seat belt for her dog? He paced through the living room to the kitchen. "The same kind who won't take a more-than-generous offer for her lousy twenty acres of land," he grumbled.

"Talking to yourself is a sure sign the aging process is taking hold."

Adam looked up to find his brother Jason regarding him with amusement. "What are you doing here?"

"I live here," Jason reminded him, his feet resting on the kitchen chair opposite him as he sat at the table, sandwich makings surrounding a rather impressive Dagwood.

"I thought you had a date with whatshername."

Jason nodded. "I do. But I thought I'd make myself a snack first."

Adam looked at the huge sandwich Jason considered a snack. "You're going to eat that and then go out to dinner?"

Jason grinned. "Yeah. So?"

"Nothing," Adam said. *"Bon appétit."*

"Thanks. Now what were you mumbling about just now?"

Adam scowled as he remembered his strange conversation with Amelia Appleberry. "I just met Miss Appleberry's niece, Amelia. She's here."

Jason nodded and chewed and swallowed. "I guess she still doesn't want to sell the place, right?"

"I'm not sure she knows what she wants," Adam said. "I wasn't sure I was following half of what she said. Something about not knowing what she wanted to do. Maybe that means she's still considering selling the place."

Jason shrugged. "I don't know. She rejected the offer I sent her from the office. Although I have to say that it was the cheeriest rejection of an offer to buy property I've ever read. What's she like in the flesh?"

Adam paused for just a few seconds, but that was a few seconds too long. Jason whistled. "Words can't express the lady's beauty?"

"I was about to say that she's just as nutty as her nutty old aunt," Adam countered quickly.

Jason smiled behind another bite of his sandwich. "So, she's a plain, rather unattractive woman."

"Oh, I wouldn't say that," Adam said, recalling the wavy brown hair; the big brown eyes; the long, long legs in the short shorts.

"When do I get to meet her?" Jason demanded after only a moment.

Adam frowned. "Why do you want to meet her?"

Jason laughed. "Any reason I shouldn't want to meet our new next-door neighbor?"

"She won't be our neighbor for long," Adam stated. "She'll sell us the land sooner or later."

Jason finished his sandwich and took a swig of a soda before saying, "You know, Adam, some brothers might make the observation that you are rather obsessed with getting your hands on the Appleberry place."

Adam pulled the refrigerator door open and looked inside, not really focusing on anything. "I'm not obsessed. But since we own the six hundred acres on this side of the Appleberry place and the four hundred acres on the other side of the Appleberry place, I just think it would be nice to have it all one piece of Larsen land."

"LarsenLand," Jason mused. "Sounds like a theme park."

Adam sighed and pulled a container of leftover spaghetti from the fridge. "You know, Jason, you could at least pretend interest in the family legacy."

"Legacy? Dad left you this place and you bought the four hundred acres from Mr. Barkley when he sold out to move to Arizona. I am just a humble small-town attorney whose brother has delusions of grandeur."

Adam tossed the plastic container into the microwave and set the timer. "I do not have delusions of grandeur. I just want to build what Dad left us into something more for my kids."

Jason's feet hit the floor as he laughed. "I hate to be the one to break it to you, brother, but you don't have any kids. Unless there's something you haven't told me."

"I intend to have kids," Adam said, adding, "someday."

His brother nodded, rising. He began to gather his sandwich makings and put them back into the fridge. "Well, since you've already declared all the women of Hillview unworthy of bearing these planned offspring, maybe you should start writing that personals ad."

Adam snorted. "You have a real gift for exaggeration, Jason. I'm convinced that you chose the right profession."

Jason shrugged. "Thank you. It's nice to know that the money on law school was not wasted. And you're just trying to change the subject. Admit it—you have dated and broken up with just about every eligible female between eighteen and forty in this town. And several from other parts of the county. There is talk that you are looking for someone that doesn't exist."

The microwave dinged and Adam used the opportunity to ignore his brother's remarks. He couldn't deny that he had dated quite a few women, or that none of them had been right for him. He didn't want to admit that he was beginning to doubt that there was a woman who was right for him.

Jason, mercifully, didn't press the issue. "I have to go. I'll see you later."

With that, Jason left and Adam sat down to eat his leftover spaghetti, wondering if he really ever would meet the woman who was perfect for him. Lately, he'd begun to think that perhaps he should reorder his priorities.

He really didn't have that many, he insisted to himself. And some were simply nonnegotiable. She had to be attractive and reasonably fit and intelligent and have a good sense of humor. Someone who grew up in the country would be a plus. Farm life wasn't easy, and city people often found it too harsh. She had to love children and animals. He wanted children, and the farm was overrun with animals.

His thoughts jumped to Amelia Appleberry and her dog with its seat belt. She obviously loved animals.

Adam's fork paused, hanging in midair over his plate as he frowned at the direction his thoughts had taken. Amelia Appleberry might be attractive and she might love animals, but Adam doubted that she was all that intelligent, at least judging from the nutty conversation he'd had with her. She didn't seem to be quite hinged.

Still, those legs . . .

Amelia climbed down out of the van and surveyed her new home. It was a fairly typical two-story farmhouse with a wraparound porch and dormer windows.

It was painted white with blue shutters, and Amelia

sighed. It was just as she remembered it from her last visit three years ago, right after she graduated from college. She'd spent a weekend with Aunt Gracie before going to Milwaukee to begin the first in a long line of dead-end jobs.

"Well, now I have some time to think," she told no one in particular. A bark from the van turned her around. "Oh, sorry, guys. I swear I didn't forget about you. I was just thinking about all the thinking I'm going to be able to do here."

She released Junior from his seat belt and the dog leaped down and immediately started to sniff every blade of grass, every shrub, and every tree within whiffing distance. She pulled Fife's carrier out and set it on the ground before opening his little door. The tiny Chihuahua took a few tentative steps out and then just stood there, unsure of what to do next.

Amelia left him to contemplate his next move. She retrieved her purse and the keys to the house and, after pulling Olga's carrier out of the van, went up the porch to the house. She unlocked the door and went inside. The house was faintly musty smelling, but not too bad.

"Okay, sweetie, here we go."

She opened the door and the cat shot out of the carrier, disappearing into the back of the house. Amelia smiled. "I don't blame you. If I'd been cooped up for hours in a dinky space like that, I'd be ready to cut loose as well."

It took several trips to get the other two cats, the dogs, Zilla the iguana, Kojak the cockatiel, and the cage containing her white mice—Larry, Curly, and Moe—into the house.

Just as she returned to the van to get her suitcases, she

heard the crunching sound of someone walking on the gravel drive. She looked around the end of the van and saw an older couple approaching.

"Hello there," the man boomed at her. "I'm Ned Winslow and this is my wife Nan. We have the place across the road. You must be Gracie's niece."

Amelia smiled at the twinkly-eyed man. "Yes, I am. My name's Amelia. It's nice to meet you both." She shook hands with them, noting how incredibly soft Nan's hands were.

"Oh, that's because of the cheese, dontcha know?" Nan informed her.

Amelia remembered the sign. "Right. The Taxidermy and Cheese Emporium. You make your own cheese?"

"Oh, sure," Nan enthused. "Been doing it for forty years now.

"One of these days she'll get it right," Ned cracked. Then cackled over his joke. Nan just looked at him and sighed.

"He loves jokes like that. After a while, you'll get used to him. Can we help you move in, dearie?"

Amelia blinked in surprise. "Oh, no, you don't have to do that. And besides, I don't have much."

Ned waved her aside and strode to the back of the van, pulling a suitcase out. "No trouble a'tall. Glad to have someone living here. Sure do miss Gracie though. She was a cutup, I don't mind saying."

Amelia smiled. "Yes, she was. I miss her, too."

Fifteen minutes later the van was empty and her meager belongings were piled in the living room. Nan surveyed the room, and especially the animals. "What's with the menagerie, dearie? You got a Dr. Doolittle complex or something?"

"Or something," Amelia laughed. "I understand that I now have several other animals, thanks to Aunt Gracie."

Ned nodded. "That's right. There're the horses and the billy goat and that old cow."

"Have you seen them yet?" Nan asked.

Amelia shook her head. "No. I know that someone has been taking care of them for the past few weeks, but I haven't had a chance to get up here until now."

Ned went to the front door and opened it. "Well, we've been taking care of them when we could. Gracie didn't trust too many people where her animals were concerned. The Larsen boy next door came over and did the grunt work. Cleaning out the stalls and forking the hay around. I'm too old for that now."

Amelia grinned at Ned calling Adam Larsen a "boy." He'd looked pretty grown up to her. But to a man of seventy or more, like Ned, a man in his early thirties was probably still a boy.

"Let's go meet and greet the wildlife, shall we?" Ned declared and walked out, apparently assuming the two women were right behind him. Which they were.

Amelia followed the older couple out into the yard and continued across it as Ned made for the barn. It wasn't exactly dilapidated, Amelia decided, generously giving the slightly sagging building the benefit of the doubt. It had charm, she thought. Although some new hinges here and there, a fresh coat of paint, and a new roof would go a long way toward perking up its spirits.

Ned reached the barn door and pulled it open. "Nan and I have been coming over and letting the horses out for exercise and the cow and goat to graze. Sometimes it's a bit of a chore getting the cow to come back, though. Might want to keep that in mind. There's a chicken coop right alongside the barn over there." He pointed to the far side of the barn where the outline of a thin door could be seen. "Better watch out for that bantam rooster if you go in there. He's a weird one."

They made their way to the stalls where two Arabian horses and a cow stood impatiently, shifting on their legs. Ned opened the first stall and Nan the second. The horses shied a bit, then took the opportunity to trot out into the corral through the open door.

Ned went to the other end of the barn and opened that door. Through it, Amelia could see the gently rolling hills of the rest of her aunt's—no, she reminded herself again, it was now *her*—property. The cow didn't care whose property it was. She slowly strolled through the barn and out the doors, the bell around her neck making an echoing clamor until she got outside.

"So, if the cow wanders off what do I do to stop her?"

Nan shrugged. "Nothing. Just go and get her . . . and hope she doesn't get through the fence and into one of the Larsen fields."

That didn't exactly sound encouraging to Amelia, but maybe the cow was just looking for companionship or something. She'd have to monitor the situation.

Amelia turned to look at the end stall, where the door had been taken off. A tethered goat lay on some hay, slowly munching some of his bedding and regarding her through unblinking eyes.

"He has to be tied up all the time," Nan told her, "because he's small enough to get through most of the fencing."

Ned laughed. "Yep. And you have to watch out for the little so-and-so. He's a butt-er."

"A butter?" Amelia felt she'd lost the thread of the conversation.

Nan nodded. "He butts a lot. Sneaky, too. Don't turn your back on him. We usually take him out back and put him in the pen next to the pigpen. He can run around in there and you don't have to worry about explaining the goat-horn bruises on your backside."

Amelia nodded, then asked, "Pigpen?"

Ned started for the back of the barn. "Oh, sure. There's only two of them, for the moment."

Before she could ask what he meant, he was gone, Nan right on his heels. Amelia hurried to catch up. She found them leaning over the wooden rails of a pigpen, looking down at its inhabitants. She joined them, stepping up onto the lower rail and leaning over the upper.

The two pigs lay in the mud, enjoying the shade of a nearby elm tree. "Sadie there should be giving you a litter of piglets in a week or so," Ned stated.

Amelia stared at him. Piglets. "Sadie's pregnant?"

"Very," Nan informed her.

"Well, I guess that's good. Am I supposed to do anything?"

Ned shrugged his bony shoulders. "Nah. In nature, it's usually best to just keep out of the way."

Amelia sighed. "I suppose I could do that." She hoped she was up to this summer.

"Oh, dear. Ned, it's almost two o'clock."

Ned looked at Nan and nodded. They both turned to

Amelia. Ned started toward the other end of the barn. "Yep. Got an appointment at two."

Nan smiled at Amelia and waggled a finger at her. "Now, if you need anything, anything at all, you just call. We're in the book."

Amelia waved as the elderly couple made their way up the driveway to the road. Junior loped across the yard and sat in front of her, his tongue lolling out the side of his mouth as he picked up one paw and waved to her. Amelia leaned down and scratched his ears.

"Well, Junior, it looks as though you're happy to be here. But the question is . . . am I?"

A short toot from a horn brought her head up and she looked down her drive to see the Winslows waving at a truck that was entering her drive. It was Adam Larsen.

Amelia's hand stilled on Junior's head and she felt her stomach tighten in anticipation. It was ridiculous, she told herself. So, he was an attractive man. So, what? She wasn't here to look for a man. She was here to look for herself and her purpose in life.

Adam stopped the truck and opened the door, jumping lightly to the ground in front of her. He looked back toward the Winslows and a wry smile teased his lips. Amelia found herself staring at those lips as he spoke.

"I see Ned and Nan stopped by. They're a little . . . eccentric . . . but really nice people."

Amelia managed to shift her gaze to his eyes before she was caught staring. "Um, yes, they seem so. They said that you've been helping care for the animals since my aunt passed away."

He nodded, the smile still in place. Amelia thought it seemed as if he thought something was funny, but wasn't sharing it with her. "Yes, I've been helping out. Miss Appleberry left me a few small gifts in her will, along with a letter requesting that I take care of things until you showed up to take over the running of the place."

Amelia wasn't sure how to take this. "Aunt Grace mentioned you in the will? Oh, yes, I remember now. You were the one she left the mystery trunk to."

Adam pushed his baseball cap back and then readjusted it atop his thick hair. "Uh, right."

"What's in it?"

He looked at her for a moment, then shrugged. "I don't know."

"You don't know?"

"I haven't really looked for the trunk. It seemed like a weird bequest."

Amelia smiled broadly, thinking about her aunt. "Well, I think you should find it and open it. How can you stand the suspense?"

Adam sighed and shoved his hands in his back pockets, causing his cotton shirt to pulled tautly across his well-muscled chest. Amelia just managed to keep her mouth from dropping open in admiration.

"Suspense? Maybe I'm just putting off the inevitable, but I have the feeling that your aunt left me an empty trunk with some bizarre instructions on what to put in it to make my life better."

Amelia tilted her head to one side and looked at him. "I think you knew my aunt pretty well."

Adam closed his eyes for a moment, then opened them and looked at her. "I wouldn't say that. I have been trying to get her to sell me this place for the last five years, and I think she would've sooner or later."

Amelia laughed. "I doubt it. Aunt Grace loved this place.

"I know," Adam conceded. "But you have to understand that I love this land, too. And I already own the land that surrounds this place."

"Really?" Now she understood why he was so adamant about buying the place. "So you want to expand your empire?"

Adam frowned. "It's hardly an empire."

"Still, you want to expand it," she said.

He nodded. "I guess so. I'd like to see my land as one continuous piece of property instead of two pieces interrupted by . . ."

"The Appleberry Place?" Amelia ventured. Adam nodded, a hopeful look in his blue eyes. She almost wished she didn't have to disappoint him, but she shook her head. "Sorry, but it looks like the Appleberry place is going to continue to interrupt your property. I'm really not interested in selling. I mean, I just got here."

She thought she saw the hope in his eyes harden, but Junior barked and she looked down to see him trot over to the porch. A tiny yip came from the other side of the screen door.

Amelia turned to walk up the steps. "Why don't you come in and look for the trunk? I need to check on Fife and the three sisters."

Adam followed her, but stopped just as she opened the screen door. *"The Three Sisters?* As in the Russian play by Chekov?"

Amelia turned, surprised. "Yes. Olga, Masha, and Irina. Are you a fan of Chekov?"

Adam shrugged. "I wouldn't say that. But I read the play in college."

Amelia nodded as she opened the door and held it open for Junior. Fife stood just inside the door. He saw Adam cross the threshold and began growling. Suddenly, he launched himself at the interloper and attached his tiny jaws to Adam's pant leg. The thick denim barely moved.

Adam looked down, then up at Amelia. "This your guard dog?"

Amelia laughed. "He thinks he's vicious." She looked down at the dog, which was still growling and tugging at the jeans. "Fife, stop that. You might hurt yourself."

The dog disentangled himself and walked stiff legged to stand just behind Amelia, next to Junior. Amelia smiled. "Good dog, Fife."

"Fife?"

"Yes, I thought he looked like Barney Fife."

Adam smiled then, really smiled, and Amelia felt her stomach flip-flop. She suddenly wondered what his laugh sounded like.

Just then one of the three sisters streaked by, disappearing behind a packing box. Their attention shifted to the parlor, where the boxes were stacked and the animals had been temporarily parked.

"What the—"

Amelia saw his eyes widen as he took in the room with the haphazardly placed boxes and the various animals on top of them.

"I told you before that I had a menagerie."

"Did you? I thought that the dogs and cats were the menagerie."

Amelia shrugged. "I just love animals and can't resist taking them in when they need me."

Adam peered at the mantel over the fireplace where Zilla lounged. "A lizard needed you?"

"Zilla was abandoned by her owners when they moved, and no one else wanted her," Amelia explained. "The same thing happened to Junior."

Adam left the iguana and walked over to peer into the box with the mice cage. "What's with the mice? They look weird."

Amelia nodded. "They're blind. They were given to me by someone who rescued them from a lab."

His head came up as he looked at her over the cage. "You have three blind mice?"

"I know. It seems absurd, but really—" Amelia sighed as Adam walked over to a covered birdcage. She wanted to warn him as he pulled the cover off, but was curious about how he would react.

"Not as absurd as a bald bird."

On the large center perch of the cage sat a white cockatiel, missing its head plumage, as well as many of its other feathers.

"That's Kojak. He has some sort of weird bird-feather disease and it causes his feathers to fall out. But he's getting better. I think."

Adam just shook his head at the pathetic, feather-impaired bird. "You got any other problem animals?"

Amelia frowned. "They aren't problems. They just needed me. And I think I needed them in a way. Nature has a way of leading you to what you need."

He looked up at her then, and Amelia felt her mouth

go dry. For the first time in her life, she couldn't think of a thing to say.

Adam looked away first as he replaced the cover on Kojak's cage. "Well, I guess I should be getting back."

He started for the door, but was attacked by Fife again before he could take more than a few steps. Amelia sank down in front of him and disentangled her errant pet. She made the mistake of looking up at him. Raw desire flared at her from his deep blue eyes and she rose on shaky legs, determined to get him out of her house so she could put more than a few feet of distance between them.

"I'll stop by tomorrow morning to check on the animals," he said, as he made his way to the door. "If you want," he added, stopping abruptly.

Amelia almost ran into his broad back. "Uh, sure. Until I get the, uh, hang of things."

He nodded and headed out to his truck. Amelia thought he seemed to be in a hurry. She stood on the porch, holding Fife, who still growled, and waved. "Thanks, Adam. For stopping by."

Adam practically jumped into the cab of the truck and started the engine. His left hand waved to her from the window. "You're welcome," he said. "I'll see you later."

With that he fairly peeled out of her driveway. Amelia was surprised she didn't get sprayed with gravel.

"I think Adam Larsen could be trouble," she told Fife absently. "I think he might want more than just this farm."

She watched the truck until it turned onto the road and disappeared from her view. "But he wants the farm more," she told herself. Why did saying that make her feel so sad?

TWO

Adam woke before his alarm had a chance to go off at five a.m. He stared at the ceiling as the first shadowy gray splinters of light began to filter through his window.

How could he convince Grace Appleberry's niece to sell him her land? Maybe he should just wait, he thought. Amelia Appleberry wasn't exactly ditsy, but she was decidedly flaky. All those weird animals, and her claim that she was here to figure out what she was supposed to do. What the hell did that mean? Maybe if he waited, she'd realize that the country was no place for a city flake like herself and she'd sell him her twenty measly acres and . . . and what?

"And nothing," he told himself as he swung his legs over the side of the bed. She was probably used to staying up late and sleeping late, he thought as he trudged to the bathroom. Once she found out what farm life was really . . .

Adam's hand paused as he reached to turn on the shower. Maybe it was just that simple, he thought, smiling to himself. Once she figured out that she was in over her head out here with the barn and the animals and all, she'd sell out to him, pack up, and leave.

Too bad about the leaving part, he thought as he

stepped under the stinging spray of the shower. Hillview was dangerously short on available women and Amelia Appleberry was the prettiest woman he'd seen in a long time.

Adam pulled his pickup to a halt in front of Amelia's house thirty minutes later. The sun had just begun to rise and he smiled to himself. She wouldn't appreciate being rousted this early, that was for sure.

He almost felt guilty as he bounded up the steps and leaned on the doorbell. But really, she had to find out what living on a farm was like, and why not from him?

When no one answered the bell after the fifth ring, Adam frowned and began knocking. Loudly. After a minute of this, he sighed in frustration. No one slept that soundly.

"Howdy, neighbor! Looking for me?"

Adam whirled around to find Amelia, fully dressed and trailing several animals, standing inside the corral, waving to him. He recovered from the surprise of seeing her up and about and strode toward her.

"I thought I'd check and see how you were doing with the livestock. They're used to being fed and cared for around now."

Amelia laughed, her brown eyes sparkling. "I found that out. They're pretty pushy, aren't they?"

Adam nodded, grudgingly admiring her good humor so early in the day. "Yes, they are. How's it going?"

She leaned over the wooden rail conspiratorially. "Actually, I'm glad you're here. I'm cool with the water, of course, but I have no idea how much feed to give them, or anything about that."

He would have been surprised if she had. "I can show you."

"I'd appreciate it," she said. "I should probably write it down and tack it to the wall so I don't forget."

Adam didn't think it would be all that difficult to recall, but he just nodded and leaned over to slip between the rails of the corral fence.

He showed her which feed to give the horses, cow, goat, and pigs and what mixtures and amounts she should be giving each. Amelia nodded and hummed a bit as he talked, but she didn't ask him to repeat anything. Adam resigned himself to checking on the animals every morning for at least a week. After all, it wasn't their fault the newest Miss Appleberry was as flaky as the last.

They walked over to look at Sadie, the pregnant sow, and Amelia stepped onto the railing to peer over it. "What do I do with baby pigs?"

Adam looked at her for a moment before answering carefully, "Well, that depends. You could keep them and raise them. Or you could sell them right after they're weaned."

She nodded, watching the sow, then her eyes came back to settle on him. "Raise them for what? Bacon bits?"

Adam hadn't expected such calm frankness, but he nodded. "Well, yes. Hogs are raised for food. They aren't good for much else. The occasional football, maybe"

After the bacon bits comment, Adam felt the pigskin reference allowable. He hoped he hadn't misread her. If she started railing at him about the injustices humankind rained down upon the animal world . . .

"I suppose that's the reality of it," she said slowly.

Adam nodded. If she went all freaky on him, he wasn't sure what he would do. "That it is," he said, deciding that the less he said, the less likely she was to blame him for whatever she felt was wrong with the world.

"I'm a vegetarian, personally," she said and then looked at him.

"Well, I'm not," he admitted.

"That's okay," she said with a small smile that made Adam wonder what she was really thinking. "We all evolve at our own pace."

"Evolve?" Adam scowled at her.

"Well," she said with a shrug as she climbed down from the railing and took a step away from it, "people evolve within themselves just as humans evolved over millions of years. If you believe in the evolution theory."

"And you don't?"

Amelia took a few steps toward the barn, then halted and turned to face him. "I didn't say that. There's a lot of unexplained theory in it, but that's what the scientists say about creationism. It's all pretty complicated, isn't it?"

He could only nod. What in the world had she just said? And why did it sort of make sense in a nonsensical way?

Spotting a piece of frayed rope on the ground, he leaned over to pick it up and before he could straighten he heard a gasp and heard Amelia yell, "Oohhh, Adam, look—" but before she could finish the sentence, he felt a really hard smack against his behind that sent him sprawling forward in the dirt.

Amelia, at his side immediately, tried to help him up.

"I'm so sorry. I didn't even see him coming until it was too late."

Adam turned to see the goat standing a few feet away, munching some grass at the edge of the enclosure and blinking at him with unrepentent eyes. Then he got himself to his feet and brushed off his dusty jeans.

"It's all right. I regret to say, it's not the first time this has happened. I'm usually more careful. I guess I was just . . . distracted."

Not exactly a stellar performance to impress the new Appleberry woman with his professional attitude and competency as a farmer and businessman. How was he supposed to convince her to sell him her land when he looked like a doofus?

Then she began scolding the goat. "Bad goat," she said to the uncaring creature. "What's your name, anyway? I can see why they make you stay in your stall, tied up. You really have to learn some manners. Then you can come out and enjoy the sunshine and frolic in the pasture. If you promise to at least try, you'll really be so much happier."

Adam just stared at her. She really was nuts. The goat seemed to be ignoring her. She picked up his tether and escorted him back to his stall in the barn.

"I'm sorry. Really. I have no idea how he got loose."

"Don't worry about it," Adam said. "Worse things have happened to me." That was the truth, he thought.

"Would you like to stay for breakfast?"

Adam surprised himself when he nodded. "Sure. If it's no trouble." He then thought about what a vegetarian might eat and wondered how he might get out of it.

Amelia smiled and turned toward the barn again. "No, of course not. Do you like blueberry muffins?"

Blueberry muffins. Couldn't kill him with those, he figured. Besides, he could always go home and eat a real breakfast.

An hour later, filled with blueberry muffins, scrambled eggs, orange juice, and even some soy substitute sausages that he didn't really like but that weren't totally repulsive, Adam realized that he'd lost a perfect opportunity to press his case for her selling out to him. He'd forgotten. How could he have forgotten?

It was Amelia, he thought. She was too distracting.

She placed all the breakfast dishes in the sink and turned to rummage through a drawer. A minute later she returned to the table, where Adam sat sipping coffee, with a pad of paper and a pencil.

"I want to make sure I write down all the feeding instructions," she said, and then proceeded to rattle off his instructions verbatim as she wrote them down.

"You have a good memory" was all he could think of to say.

Amelia nodded. "I know. It's the only way I made it through school."

"Where did you go?"

She pushed the pad away and looked up. "I went to high school in a suburb of Milwaukee, then I went to Wisconsin."

"In Madison?"

She nodded.

Adam was impressed. The University of Wisconsin at Madison was the premiere university in the state and one of the top universities in the Midwest.

"What did you study?"

Now she frowned. "Well, I couldn't really decide, so I just sort of stayed in the liberal arts curriculum."

Adam smiled. "What's the matter? Couldn't you decide what you wanted to be when you grew up?"

"Actually, I couldn't," she said softly. "I still can't."

Amelia saw the confusion in his eyes, so she offered an explanation before he could ask for one. "I just assumed that once I was in college something would leap out at me—this is what I'm supposed to do with my life!"

"But nothing leaped at you?" Adam didn't laugh at her, and for that, Amelia was grateful.

She shook her head. "No. And so I worked my way through college. Waitressing, retail, office work. I volunteered at hospitals and animal shelters . . ."

"You seem to like animals," he said, Amelia thought rather diplomatically.

"I love animals," she said. "That was my problem. I loved them too much. I couldn't stand to see them in cages. They were so sad. I'd just cry all day, and I ended up with headaches and a new pet every other week. My landlord finally said I had to either stop bringing more animals home or get out."

"So, what did you do?"

"I quit my job. Of course, I also moved. He really didn't understand about the animals. So, I moved to Chicago. I figured maybe a bigger city would show me all sorts of interesting things to do with my life."

Adam finished his coffee and nodded. "Did it?"

"Yes. And no. More short-term jobs, but no insight. I began to fear that I'd never find my purpose in life."

"So," he said slowly, "now you've found your purpose?"

Amelia tried to read his expression, but he seemed to be deliberately neutral.

"No, but at least now I've found a place to think about what I want and maybe to make some decisions."

"That place being here?"

Adam seemed rather quiet. After a moment she said, "I was really surprised when my Aunt Gracie left me this place when she passed away."

"You didn't spend much time here, did you?" Adam asked. Amelia couldn't tell if he were merely curious or if he were subtly accusing her of something.

"Not really. A couple of weekends here and there. I always loved it here, though. And Aunt Gracie and I had struck up a sort of correspondence over the last couple of years. I probably learned more about her through her letters than I ever did when I was actually here."

"Why don't I ever remember seeing you before?"

His question surprised her only because she'd been thinking the same thing. "Um . . . I don't know. Maybe because I never really stayed very long. Mostly weekend trips with my parents when I was in high school."

Adam nodded. "I was probably away at college then. I went to Wisconsin myself."

"Really? When did you graduate?"

"Eight years ago."

Amelia smiled. "That's just about when I was getting there. What did you study?"

"Agriculture," he said.

Amelia felt like an idiot. "Of course. You're a farmer.

"That's not necessarily a given. My brother and I were both sons of a farmer. He is now a lawyer."

"And you're upholding the family tradition?"

Adam's lips curved into a small smile as he tugged absently on his earlobe. "I guess you could say that. I love the land and the whole reap-sow philosophy of a farmer. It's very satisfying to plant seeds and see the crops grow and mature and then to know that they're an essential part of life as food for hundreds of people."

Amelia nodded as she thought about what he said. "Farming," she said softly. "I've never tried that."

"What?"

She refocused her gaze on his face. He looked at her with what looked like dread. Couldn't be, Amelia thought. He doesn't know me well enough to dread something I might say.

"Farming. Maybe that's what I was meant to do."

"Forgive me for being blunt, but you have no idea what you're talking about. Farming is hard work. And it's risky. Crops can fail because of weather or insects or just because you didn't water or fertilize them properly. And the soil has to be cared for and—"

"I didn't say I thought it would be easy," Amelia told him, a bit put out that he thought she would automatically fail. Just as she had failed at everything else. But he couldn't know that. Or could he? She'd told him too much, probably. She usually did. She'd lost more potential boyfriends that way.

Amelia paused at the sink as she was about to put a plate into the water. Boyfriend? Did she think of Adam Larsen as a potential boyfriend? Why did that label seem so . . . high school? And why was she even thinking it?

He was just a friendly neighbor. Besides, she didn't need romantic distractions. She was here to contemplate her future career choices, not to get involved with anyone.

Even if he were attractive and sexy—and really filled out his faded jeans . . .

". . . and that's not even taking into consideration all the maintenance costs for barns and transportation costs for delivering the crops . . . What?"

Adam stopped talking and looked at her expectantly. Amelia suddenly realized that she had been staring openly at him with who knows what kind of expression. If his wary expression was anything to go by, she thought, it must have been enough to make him wonder what she was thinking about. But she couldn't very well tell him she'd been mentally undressing him.

So, she just looked back at him and baldly said, "What what?"

His brows drew together in a confused, yet somewhat disbelieving frown. "You just seemed to be . . . ignoring me."

Amelia shook her head. "Oh, no. I could never do that. I mean, my mind may have wandered a bit, but I definitely wasn't ignoring you. What were you saying?"

He just stared at her again, and Amelia fought the grimace she felt inside as she thought about what she'd just said. *He thinks I'm an idiot,* she thought. *And he probably isn't far from wrong.*

"I was just saying that farming is very hard and very expensive and there are no guarantees—"

"Well," Amelia said, glad that she knew where she was again, "there isn't much in life that does have guarantees, right?"

She continued to clear the table of the breakfast dishes, grateful for something to keep her hands occupied, if not her brain.

"No," he agreed after a moment. "But you aren't really serious about farming this land, are you?"

Amelia stopped at the sink and slowly set the dishes down before turning to face him. "I don't know. It might be something that I'd be good at."

Adam rose and slowly pushed his chair in before looking at her again. "I don't want to sound sexist or anything, but a woman alone trying to farm twenty acres of land . . . well . . . have you ever driven a tractor before?"

Amelia felt like a fool. "No, I haven't. But I wouldn't want to start out with the whole twenty acres. I mean, I'd have to learn more about it first. What to plant, when to plant, how much. That sort of thing."

He nodded and Amelia was glad he didn't make fun of her. "Those are all important things to think about. Maybe you should just start out with the vegetable garden Miss Appleberry always kept. It's only about half an acre, but it could give you a sense of what growing food is like."

Amelia brightened at his suggestion. "That's a great idea. I'll start working on it this afternoon."

He didn't say anything for a moment, then, "Well, I should be going. Thanks for breakfast. It was really good. And if you need any help with the garden, just let me know."

With that, he strode through the hallway to the front door and was in his truck before Amelia could offer to see him out.

She held up her hand in a weak wave as he turned his

truck around and drove up the drive. He was certainly a difficult man to try and figure out, she thought absently. But his idea about the garden was just what she needed. And she'd do it without asking for any help. He probably already thought she was completely useless out here.

Or did he? He wanted to buy her land. He made no secret about that. But just how badly did he want it?

Amelia felt something brush against her leg and looked down to find Masha winding herself around her leg. She bent down and picked up the calico cat and held her to her chest.

"Well, he's not going to get it," she whispered to the cat, who didn't seem to be particularly interested in anything but the pleasures of a good ear-scratching. "I have to sort out my life, and I'm not leaving here until I do."

With that she put Masha on the floor and stalked off toward the back of the house, where she thought maybe she had seen some gardening tools. Or was it the shed?

It was the shed.

Amelia found the tools after she left the house and took a cursory tour of the garden. Small by country standards, the half-acre plot seemed huge to Amelia. But maybe it just seemed big because it was currently empty, she reasoned, taking in the shriveled remains of Aunt Gracie's garden.

She realized that she didn't even know where to begin.

"Maybe I should have asked Adam more questions," she muttered to herself. "Something along the lines of— are you seeing anyone?"

Shaking her head to clear her wayward thoughts,

ADAM'S KISS   37

Amelia tried to concentrate on the garden. But she had no idea where to begin.

Junior loped up to her and sat down, his tongue hanging out. Amelia looked at his openly adoring face and smiled. "You know, Junior, just because I haven't done this before doesn't mean I won't be good at it, right?"

Junior barked happily. Of course, he always barked happily, no matter what she said to him. She looked back at the bedraggled garden and wondered how she would conquer its mysteries. Then she brightened. "I know. I'll just get a couple of books on gardening from the local library." Junior barked happily.

Amelia looked down at him, feeling happier herself. "There isn't anything you can't learn from books." A completely logical idea, she thought proudly as she headed into the house to get her keys.

A rogue image of Adam Larsen floated into her mind. "Well, almost anything."

Adam looked up when he heard a car passing by and saw Amelia Appleberry's white van trundling toward town. "Farming," he said, shaking his head. She was nutty; that's all there was to it. She had absolutely no idea what she was talking about.

"Then again," he said thoughtfully as he turned back toward his barn where several workers were already well into the day's labor, "once she finds out how much time, effort, and sweat it takes, maybe she'll give up and sell out."

And leave town.

Adam frowned to himself when he felt a pang of regret

over that eventuality. Maybe she could just move to town, he thought, and then nodded to himself. Why not?

"Whadja say, boss? Why not what?"

Adam looked up quickly, unaware that he'd entered the barn muttering to himself. "Nothing, Harry," he said quickly. "Just got a lot on my mind. By the way, do we have any vegetable or herb seeds anywhere around?"

Harry, a wiry man with over thirty years of farmhand experience, looked over at Joe, whose salt-and-pepper eyebrows were raised in an expression of disbelief. Adam looked from one to the other and realized that they both looked surprised, and a bit confused.

"Uh . . . sure . . . maybe," Joe managed.

Harry just snorted after a moment and said, "Whaddya gonna do? Raise cucumber samwiches?"

Joe thought this was inordinately funny. Adam sighed. "What? What's wrong with a vegetable garden? My mother used to have one."

Both men sobered at the mention of the late Mrs. Larsen. Joe even took off his hat briefly. "That she did," he said reverently. "Your mother had a way with that garden, she did. Didn't she, Harry?"

Harry nodded. "That she did, Joe. That she did."

Adam, used to the high level of respect, sometimes it seemed more like awe, that the two older men felt toward his late mother, paused before continuing. "Actually, I was thinking that we might give the seeds to our new neighbor."

The two men were pulled out of their reverie by this statement. Joe slapped his baseball cap with the tractor logo on it back on his head and scowled. "That Appleberry woman was nothing but trouble."

Harry cackled at him. "You're just mad 'cause she turned you down every time you asked her to the picture show.

Joe bristled and turned to face Harry. "I seem to recall that you weren't all that successful with her yourself."

"Oh, yeah?"

Adam waved his arms to get their attention. "Hey, guys. I think it's safe to say that the recently departed Miss Appleberry didn't really like any of us, all right? I just thought it would be a nice gesture to offer the new Miss Appleberry a—well, a housewarming gift, sort of . . . you know, to show there aren't any hard feelings."

Harry and Joe looked at each other. Harry took off his hat and scratched his wispy-haired head. "Hard feelings over what?"

"Well, she's still refusing to sell the place to me."

Joe chuckled. "I s'pose you went right over there and just offered to buy the place the first day she's here."

Adam didn't think he was going to like where this conversation was headed, but he nodded. "Yes. So?"

Harry and Joe began cackling as if on cue. "Boy," Harry announced, "you sure didn't learn much about women at that college you went to, did you?"

"I'm thinking he didn't," Joe chimed in. "You shoulda waited, stood back, got the lay of the land, used the old Larsen charm on her."

The old Larsen charm. Adam just shook his head. "You know, I think you two have worked here too long. My father and brother brainwashed you."

Joe stiffened at the imagined slur. "Now don't you go bad-mouthing your Pa. He was a good man, George was."

Adam nodded. "I know he was, Joe. But you gotta

admit . . . oh, never mind. Listen, all I want to know is if we have some seeds we can give to Amelia Appleberry for her to plant in her garden. She wants to try out farming."

This sent the two older men into gales of laughter. After they'd quieted, Adam said, "I know, that's what I thought. But I figured, if she wants to find out about farming, then we should help her out."

Harry looked at him slyly. "And when she finds out she's bit off more than she can chew, she'll sell out and get out?"

Adam just shrugged. Joe nodded thoughtfully and tugged at a few scraps of beard adorning his weathered face. "What if she likes it?"

Adam stared at the two men for a moment. Then they both burst into gales of laughter and walked away, cackling about how interesting this summer was going to be.

Interesting wasn't a word Adam would've chosen.

The Hillview Public Library had quite a gardening section. Perennials. Annuals. Groundcover. Landscaping. They even had books on topiary and bonsai trees.

"Ahh," she sighed as she spied the section devoted to vegetable gardening. There must have been two dozen different books on the subject. Using a time-honored method of decision-making, Amelia closed her eyes, turned around, and pointed. She opened her eyes and pulled the book she'd pointed to off the shelf. *Vegetable and Herb Gardening Made Easy.*

"Sounds perfect," she murmured and started for the exit.

After getting her library card and explaining to the curious librarian about how she'd inherited her Aunt Gracie's property, she headed outside.

Before she could make it to her van, she found herself drawn to a pitiful sight. A dog—a puppy, really—was tied to the bike rack outside the library. There was plenty of shade and it wasn't very warm yet, but the dog looked so unhappy that Amelia's heart went out to him. He was chewing on his rope leash, and looked as if he'd made some progress.

"Hey, fella, what's the matter? Did someone leave you out here while they went in to get a book?"

The scrappy little terrier mix looked up at her and wagged his tail, the leash still in his mouth. Amelia looked at the chewed leash and clucked her tongue. "You shouldn't do that, you know. It's only there for your own good. Your person must love you very much. You shouldn't try to get away. They'll be back soon."

The dog looked up at her curiously, then abruptly sat down and dropped the leash. Amelia smiled at him and patted his head gently. "Now, doesn't that feel better?"

"Hey, whatcha doin' with Leo?"

Amelia turned to see a boy, about eight or nine, holding two library books and looking at her curiously.

"I was just talking to your dog. He's *cute.*"

The boy beamed. "I know. I just got him last week." His face clouded as he untied the dog and looked at the slightly mangled leash. "But my mom says if he doesn't stop chewing everything, I might have to give him back."

Amelia's heart went out to the boy. "I don't think it will come to that. Leo's a good dog at heart, aren't you, Leo?"

The dog wagged his tail and woofed at her. She laughed and said, "See?"

The little boy grinned and nodded. "I know. But, boy, he sure likes to chew stuff."

Amelia remembered that Junior had been the same way. "My dog used to like to chew things, too. It was usually because he was bored. Do you have any other animals?"

"No. I had to beg my mom forever just to get Leo."

"Well, maybe he just needs some friends to play with. Why don't you bring him over to my house and he can play with my dogs. Do you know where the Appleberry place is?"

The boy nodded. "Sure. Miss Appleberry was a nice old lady."

Amelia smiled. "Yes, she was. I'm her niece, Amelia Appleberry.

"I'm Matt O'Brien. I live at the end of the street over there." He pointed in the general direction of the street the library was on. "If I ask my mom, maybe she'll let me bring Leo over."

Speaking of his new friend, Matt leaned over and picked up the dog, hoisting him into the basket on the front of a bicycle. Leo seemed to like this and sat quietly.

"Tell her to come with you," Amelia suggested, aware that visiting strangers, even the niece of someone you knew, probably wasn't typical for children in Hillview.

Matt nodded as he mounted his bike. "Okay. See you later, Miss Appleberry."

With that he wheeled out of the library parking lot, Leo's ears flapping slightly in the breeze.

Amelia smiled at the sight, then turned toward her van.

She glanced down at the book as she opened the door and got in. In no time at all she'd be growing tomatoes and cucumbers and peppers and squash and beans and anything else she felt like. Maybe Adam Larsen would have some suggestions as to what she should plant.

Adam. Just thinking about his ruggedly handsome face and his blue bedroom eyes made her want to plant . . . a kiss right on his full sexy lips.

She sighed. "What Amelia wants and what Amelia gets are hardly ever the same thing, now, are they?"

It took her a moment to realize that she was talking to herself, with nary an animal in sight. She plunged the key into the ignition and started the engine, then pulled her seat belt around her.

What she needed was some good old-fashioned physical labor to help her get her mind off her neighbor. She had decisions to make about her future and they didn't include Adam Larsen. No matter how sexy and attractive he was.

"So, I'll get right to work on the garden and it'll take my mind off him. Right?" No one answered her and Amelia sighed.

Just before reaching the outskirts of town, Amelia spotted a small diner set back from the road and decided that she should stop and have lunch and maybe pick up a little of the local flavor while she was at it.

Several pickup trucks and a few cars were parked in the small parking lot. She passed between two trucks on her way to the door and, as she glanced to her right, noticed that the truck's owner had left the keys in the ignition.

A trusting community, she thought as she opened the

door and walked into the cooled interior of the diner. A dozen or so booths lined the front and side walls, and a counter with red padded stools ran the length of the interior. There were a few booths open, but Amelia decided to sit at the counter.

She sat down and pulled the small menu from between the salt and pepper shakers and a napkin dispenser and wondered if there would be anything vegetarian she could eat. It didn't surprise her to find that most of the offerings were of the burger and fries variety, but there was a grilled cheese sandwich and a BLT listed.

"What can I get for you?"

Amelia looked up at the attractive woman who stood across the counter from her, holding an order pad. "Um . . . can I get a cheese, lettuce, and tomato sandwich on whole wheat?"

The woman wrote, her eyebrows raising a bit, but then just nodded. "Sure, why not? Would you like something to drink?"

Amelia ordered a soda and the waitress hurried off to place the order, then to take another at the other end of the counter.

There was a pile of flyers on the end of the counter proclaiming the spring musical at Hillview High to be *The King and I*. Most of the people she'd known in Milwaukee and Chicago couldn't have been dragged to a high school play. But Amelia thought it looked like fun. She folded the flyer and tucked it into her pocket just as the waitress returned with her soda.

"Going to the play?"

Amelia smiled. "I think I might. It's been awhile since I went to see any live theatre."

The waitress, Dori, according to her name tag, laughed. "Well, it's live and I guess it's a form of theatre . . . kind of primitive theatre, if you know what I mean."

"Do you know someone in the production?" Amelia asked.

"It'd be a miracle in this town if I didn't know somebody in it," Dori cracked, her eyes crinkling with laughter. "My daughter's one of the parade of kids."

Amelia smiled. "Right. 'The March of the Siamese Children.' "

"Whatever. All I know is that Tiffany has blond hair and blue eyes and she's gotta have this stuff sprayed on her hair every night to make it black and it's harder than heck to get out."

"I'll bet she loves it, though."

Dori rolled her eyes. "She thinks she's Broadway bound. But you know, she is good. She can sing really good and she's been taking dance lessons for a couple of years now. Actually, I don't mind washing goop out of her hair if it means she's having a good time and learning more about the world outside Hillview."

A bell dinged and Dori held up a hand. "There's your lunch. I'll be right back."

Amelia watched as Dori deftly managed to get three people their lunches and beverages while assisting another waitress with a large order and answering the phone to take a carry-out order all in less than two minutes. Amelia's own short-lived waitressing career had been doomed by her own inability to focus in a frenzied atmosphere.

Dori slid the sandwich in front of Amelia. "There you go. Sorry about the wait."

Thinking about the few minutes she'd waited here compared to the really long waits in the trendy restaurants of Chicago, Amelia smiled. "It wasn't really a wait. You're very good at what you do."

Dori looked surprised. "Well, thanks. I don't hear that very much. Nice, though. What do you do?"

Amelia felt some of her good mood slip away. "Actually, I don't have a job."

Dori just nodded. "Oh. A stay-at-home mom? I'd love to be able to do that."

"Uh, no," Amelia stammered, "I—that is—well, to tell the truth, I don't know what I want to do with my life."

She braced herself for the blank stare and the obligatory, "I see." But Dori surprised her.

"Well, don't let it get you down. I only decided what I wanted to do when I grew up last year. I'm taking classes at the community college. I'm going to be a midwife."

Amelia leaned forward. "Really? That's wonderful. What made you decide?"

"Well, I have three kids of my own and each birth was a completely different experience. But the best by far was the one I had with a midwife. So, after thinking about it for a while and finding out what I would have to do, I decided to go back to school and do it. It's taking me about ten times as long as it should, since I'm working full time and taking care of my kids."

"But it's worth it," Amelia murmured wistfully.

"Yes, it is," Dori echoed before hurrying off to deliver more food and take more orders. Amelia sat slowly munching her sandwich and thinking about how lucky Dori was to have found her career. Then again, it had taken her three children and many years of doing other things before she'd found it. Still, it provided Amelia a glimmer of hope.

A few feet away, three young women approached the cash register as Dori returned to take away Amelia's empty plate. "Anything else I can get you?"

Amelia shook her head. "No, thank you. It was very good."

"You know, we don't get a lot of single strangers in here. If you don't think I'm being too nosy, where are you from?"

"That's all right," Amelia assured her. "Actually, I am from around here now. I'm Amelia Appleberry. I'm living in the house my Aunt Gracie left me. Perhaps you've heard of her?"

"Miss Appleberry?" Dori said, laughing. "Of course I knew her."

One of the girls at the cash register waved at Dori. "See you later, Dori."

Dori waved back. "Hey, Heather, I just found out who's staying at the Appleberry place."

Heather, a tall, pretty blonde, hurried over, trailing her two friends. "Who?"

Dori pointed at Amelia, who smiled tentatively and said, "That would be me. Amelia Appleberry. My Aunt Gracie left it to me."

Suddenly surrounded, Amelia met Heather and her friends, Brenda and Morgan.

"How long have you been here?"

"Do you have anybody helping you?"

"Are you married?"

Dori laughed and commandeered their attention. "Go

easy on her, she's new in town. She'll think we're the local '60 Minutes' interrogation squad."

"That's okay," Amelia assured them when they started to apologize. "I am new around here. I just arrived yesterday; I'm not married; it's just me and my collection of animals. And I've been very fortunate to have the man who lives next door, so to speak, come over and help out with the farm animals."

Heather chuckled. "Adam Larsen. I'll bet he was thrilled to see you."

Amelia shook her head. "What do you mean?"

"Nothing. Just that he's wanted your land forever."

If that was supposed to be news, it wasn't, Amelia thought. She just shrugged. "I know. I got a letter several weeks ago from him, and when he came over he mentioned his desire to buy it again."

"And?"

Amelia wasn't sure if it were Morgan or Brenda who asked, but she shook her head. "I told him I wasn't interested in selling."

They all seemed impressed and fell temporarily silent. Dori bustled off to care for the remains of the dwindling lunch crowd.

After a moment Heather, perched on a stool to Amelia's right, laughed. "I don't know many women around here that would've been able to say no to Adam Larsen."

Morgan and Brenda both smiled and laughed quietly. Knowingly, Amelia thought with a frown. It seemed that these women all knew something about Adam Larsen, or thought they did; and even though Amelia had just met the man, she didn't like to think that he was the town Romeo. Even if he were attractive enough to play the part.

"He seems very nice," she said politely. Unfortunately, that only brought hoots of laughter from the Hillview natives.

"Nice?" Morgan repeated. "Well, yeah, he's nice, even though he doesn't have to be. With those eyes and that body, nobody would care if he were nice or not."

"If I weren't married . . ." Brenda sighed.

Heather laughed at her friend. "You had your chance with him—just like everybody else."

Amelia blinked. "Everybody else?"

Heather shrugged. "It's a small town. There are only so many people of the opposite sex in your age range. So, by the time you're thirty"—Morgan cleared her throat in protest, but Heather ignored her—"you've pretty much gone through every available man or woman around. So, by then you're either already married or you're looking elsewhere, having run out of choices close to home."

"Really? So, are all of you married?"

"I am." Brenda sighed. "I met my husband when I was in college. So did Morgan. Heather is our only holdout. And she's dating Jason. But who knows what'll come of that?"

Heather frowned comically. "I should be insulted. But you're right. I have no idea myself."

"Who's Jason?" Amelia asked.

"Jason Larsen," Heather said. "Adam's brother. He's a lawyer."

"Oh, right. He's the one who sent me the letter. I haven't met him."

Heather smiled. "He's very cute. Like Adam. Only more buttoned down."

"Have you dated long?" Amelia suddenly realized that that was possibly a too personal question to ask someone she had just met, but Heather didn't seem to mind.

"On and off for about six years."

"She's trying for a record," Brenda cracked before looking at her watch and yelping, "Holy cow, I gotta go. I still have to do the grocery shopping before the kids get home from school. I'll see you guys later."

Morgan hurried after her, both calling out it was nice to meet her, and Amelia waved at them. Heather picked up her purse and hung it on her shoulder.

"I have to be getting back to work myself. I hope we didn't shell-shock you."

Amelia shook her head. "No, really, it was nice to meet all of you. I hope that we see each other again soon."

"No problem." Heather laughed. "It's Hillview. You'll probably see us every day. Unless you hole up at the Appleberry place with Adam Larsen." She waggled her eyebrows suggestively, but it was too funny for Amelia to take as anything other than a joke.

"I don't know about that," she said softly. "I'm really just here to figure out what I want to do with the rest of my life. I'm not looking for a man."

Dori, who'd been leaning against the counter since the other two had left, gave her a wink and a knowing grin. "But that's when you meet Mr. Right. When you aren't looking."

Amelia laughed along with them and waved as Heather left to go back to work. She then turned to Dori and said,

"I don't really know how long I'll be here in Hillview. And I really am only here to figure out my life."

Dori nodded. "I understand. I hope you don't think we were too nosy."

"Oh, no," Amelia quickly assured her. "It was nice, actually. I haven't really met anybody except Adam Larsen and the Winslows who live across the road."

Dori rolled her eyes. "Aren't they an interesting couple? That place of theirs gives me the creeps."

"I haven't seen it yet. The only place I've been besides here has been the library. I got some books on gardening. I don't suppose you know anything about gardening?"

Dori smiled. "What do you want to know?"

When she left thirty minutes later, Amelia felt more confused about the gardening thing than ever. There were just too many variables, she thought as she got back into her van. Too many choices and too much to consider. Pretty much like her life had been so far, she thought ruefully.

THREE

When Amelia arrived back at Aunt Gracie's house—she still didn't think of it as her house—she greeted her pets and then sat down to look over her book. Dori had pointed out much of what the book illustrated. There were just so many decisions to make. Choosing seeds or plants, fertilizers, how much water each plant needed, how much room to give each type of plant . . . She was barely past the table of contents and already felt doubts creeping in.

The sound of tires on gravel pulled her attention to the kitchen window and she looked out to see Adam Larsen emerging from his pickup truck, a paper bag in his hand. Just the man she needed to talk to. About the garden, she told herself.

She tried not to hurry to the front door, unable to stop herself from checking her reflection in the mirror next to the door just before he knocked. She reached for the doorknob, then stopped. What would he think if she yanked open the door as soon as he knocked? She didn't want him to think that she had nothing to do but sit around waiting for him to visit.

He knocked again, and Amelia shook her head at her inexplicable nervousness, then opened the door.

Adam stood looking at her through the screen door. He

waited a moment, then held up the bag. "I brought you a housewarming gift."

Amelia stared. Then, realizing that Adam still stood on a welcome mat that her attitude didn't seem to match, she said hurriedly, "I'm sorry. Come in. And you didn't have to do that."

He entered the house and Amelia backed into the living room, which was still filled with boxes and animal crates. "I know I didn't have to, but I got to thinking after I left this morning and I remembered that we had some seeds around that we weren't using. I thought you might like them."

Adam held the bag out and she reached for it, her fingers brushing his before he let go.

Amelia felt a rush of electricity shimmer along her skin. "I'd love them," she managed, forcing herself not to rub her tingling fingers. "What are they?"

Adam shrugged. "To tell the truth, I'm not too sure. My mother used to do the vegetable gardening for the family. After she died last year, the garden just sort of got forgotten. I found those and thought you might get some use out of them."

Amelia struggled to find a response. His mother's seeds? She couldn't think of a thing to say that wouldn't sound maudlin or weepy. "Well, thank you," she finally said, opening the bag and peeking into it eagerly. Inside were little paper envelopes. There had to be a dozen different seeds. She looked up at Adam with pleasure. "This is wonderful. I wasn't sure what I should plant. I even went to the library and got a book."

He nodded. "That could be a help. But since you said

you'd never gardened before, I figured you might like a leg up . . . so to speak."

Amelia laughed. "I hope that these help me get off to a good start. I'd just started to look at the book and it seemed so complicated for something that's supposed to be so simple."

"Growing things isn't as easy as dropping a seed in the dirt," he agreed.

Amelia nodded, then realized they were still standing in the living room, just inside the foyer, and motioned him in. "I was just about to make some tea and read about gardening," she said, "but since you're here, maybe you could answer some questions."

He hesitated, then nodded. "Okay."

They walked down the hallway to the kitchen and Amelia set the bag of seeds on a countertop as Adam sat down at the table. The gardening book still lay on the table and he pulled it toward him. The table, situated under a wide window, looked over the wraparound porch and then to the front yard. Amelia hoped he wouldn't notice that she'd been sitting here, looking at the book, and had to have seen his arrival, then acted surprised at seeing him at her front door. Or, at the very least, she hoped he wouldn't call her on it.

"Would you like some tea? Or maybe some coffee? I have both."

Adam looked up from the book. "Coffee, please. I'm not much of a tea drinker. Unless it's iced tea."

Amelia set up the coffeemaker and the water for her tea, then sat down at the table with Adam. She opened the bag and began pulling the little envelopes out. Cucumbers. Tomatoes. Squash. Beans. Lettuce. She had no idea where to begin.

"So, what do you think I should plant?"

Adam shrugged one shoulder. "That depends. Do you plan to use the garden for your own personal use or for a vegetable stand?"

"You mean, like set up a stand by the road and sell tomatoes?"

He nodded. "Sure. Some people do it because they get bumper crops of tomatoes or cucumbers; others plant extra to make a few bucks with very little more effort."

"I hadn't thought about that," Amelia admitted.

"Well, you might end up doing the vegetable stand thing anyway," he said, then hesitated before adding, "unless you know something about canning and preserving?"

Amelia sighed, the familiar feeling of impending failure creeping over her. "Well, no. Not really. I suppose most people who plant gardens do."

Adam nodded and Amelia drew in a deep breath. "Maybe I shouldn't do this," she began, her enthusiasm for the project waning in the face of her ignorance.

"I suppose you could just forget about it," Adam replied. "But then you'd never know what it's like to plant something and care for it and watch it grow."

Amelia studied him. "You really love farming, don't you?" she said softly.

"Yes, I do," he said.

"I wondered if maybe you just did it because that's what your family did. But you really love it. I think that's great."

He grinned at her and Amelia felt a curious sensation in the pit of her stomach. Sort of a quivery, fluttery feeling. She didn't have time to think more about it, when Adam said, "So do I. Even when I was a kid, I loved working with the land."

Amelia tried to match his enthusiasm and hoped she was successful. "I envy you. I've never known what I wanted to do, what I wanted to be."

He leaned forward and rested his forearms on the table, gazing at her. The intensity she glimpsed in his eyes almost made her look away, but she refused to let herself. "There's nothing wrong with taking your time to make a decision that will affect the rest of your life. Take the time and make the right decision."

A sound born of frustration threatened to strangle her. "I don't think that time alone is going to do the trick. I have to experiment. I have to try different things. I just know that when the right career comes along, I'll know it. Maybe farming is the answer. Maybe it's not. All I know is that I have to try. Because what if it were my destiny and I ignored it?"

"What if it weren't? What if it were totally wrong for you?"

She sighed. "Then at least I'd know."

She thought she actually saw understanding in his eyes. Then the kettle whistled and startled her. She turned to see that the coffee was already done. "I didn't even notice," she confessed.

Adam waved her concern away. "Don't worry about it. It's not as if it's been getting cold."

Amelia busied herself with cups and saucers, annoyed that her hands were shaking. What was it about this man that made her nervous? She'd dated before, a couple of times seriously, but never had she found herself attracted to the point of nervousness. And to a man who probably just wanted her gone. After he got her land, of course. She'd do well to remember that little piece of information.

She put his coffee in front of him and watched him put a scant teaspoon of sugar in it. She put sugar and a bit of milk in her tea and stirred it. Too much, she realized, as the spoon clattered against the cup.

"So," he said, gallantly pretending not to notice her fidgety fingers, "are you ready to plant a garden?"

Amelia paused, surprised by her own response. He might not have a clue what that sentence meant to her, but she wasn't afraid to try anymore. She felt a huge veil of indecision lifting from around her and it filled her with hope.

They stood at the edge of the garden, surveying the dead plants among the weeds that threatened to take over the entire quarter-acre plot. Amelia couldn't believe that her little old aunt had tended such a large garden year after year. She looked over at Adam. "What do I do first?"

"First, you have to clear the land; then you have till it; then you have to fertilize it; then you have to seed it; then you have to tend it."

She swallowed, but nodded as nonchalantly as she could. "Okay. But I thought clearing the land referred to cutting down trees and getting rid of big rocks."

Adam laughed. "Well, it does mean that. But it also means just clearing away the dead plants and weeds. Most people just till the dead plants into the soil so it acts as sort of a natural fertilizer."

"Recycling," Amelia said, grateful for a concept she understood. "Okay."

"Right. Of course, that's usually only if you have a Rototiller or some other type of motorized equipment."

Amelia knew with a sinking feeling what was coming. "I suppose Aunt Gracie didn't believe in motorized equipment."

Adam shoved his hands in his back pockets and rocked back on his heels. "Nope. She liked to do everything the hard way."

It was a daunting prospect, but Amelia knew there was only one way to find out if she had a talent for farming, and that was to experience it totally. "Then I guess I'd better get started," she said, and dropped to her knees at the edge of the garden and started pulling weeds and dead plants.

Adam hunkered down next to her. "You don't have to do it this way, you know. I have a small tiller I could bring over and have this whole thing done in an hour or less."

As attractive as that offer sounded, Amelia shook her head. "If I'm going to find out about farming, then I should approach it in the most basic, simplistic manner."

"You're just creating a lot of unneccessary work for yourself."

She couldn't argue with him there, she thought as she wrestled a plant from the ground and then shook the loose soil from its dead roots. "Maybe. But learning something the hard way usually makes you appreciate the accomplishment all the more."

"You're as stubborn as Miss Appleberry was, aren't you?"

She tossed the next handful of dead plant onto her barely there pile. "I *am* Miss Appleberry, you know."

Adam grumbled something about traits running in families, then sighed. "Look, I have to go and take care of some things at my place. Take my advice. Don't overdo it. Make sure you take time to stretch your muscles and don't forget to use some sunscreen."

Amelia nodded. "All right."

"I mean it," he said. "I wouldn't want you to get sunburned or succumb to heatstroke or sunstroke."

"It's not that hot out," she reminded him.

"Trust me," he warned. "It may not feel hot, but in just a few hours it can do a lot of damage."

Amelia stood up and faced him. "All right. I'll go put on some sunscreen."

"And a hat."

She just rolled her eyes and headed for the side door. Adam got into his truck and turned it around. Amelia watched him drive off, shielding her eyes from the sun. It was then she realized that the sun was brighter than she'd thought. She jerked her hand away just as she saw Adam pointing to his own head. He was pushy, she thought, but it was nice to have someone who could be pushy on her behalf. That hadn't happened in a very long time.

Several hours later, with the sun beginning to set, Amelia still crept along on her hands and knees in the garden, wondering what had possessed her to turn down Adam's offer of a few quick passes with his tiller. Her fingernails were caked with dirt, as was most of the rest of her. Her jean shorts were covered with dirt and there were smudges on her pale green tee-shirt. There was dirt in her sneakers and she was sure that there was dirt in her hair—underneath the hat she'd put on at Adam's insistence. But now that the sun was going down . . . she tossed the hat onto the grass.

She'd only taken one real break. That was to chase down the cow, which had been trying to trample down part of the fence and get to Adam Larsen's bean field. At least Amelia thought they were beans. She'd herded the cow, the horses, and the goat back into their stalls and headed back to her gardening chore.

Junior and Fife had spent the afternoon lying about in the shade and running around the yard. Now they lay together at the edge of the garden, watching her.

She knew she should've quit at the halfway point and finished the job the next day, but since she was already dirty and she really didn't want to have to do this anymore, she'd decided to press on.

There was just a bare glow of sunlight when she finished clearing the plot and rose stiffly to survey her work. There was a ring around the plot of the weeds and dead plants she'd pulled and tossed away from the soil. She'd deal with those tomorrow, she told herself.

"I did it," she said aloud. Fife rose unsteadily and ventured to the edge of the dirt before stopping. Junior got up and stretched and looked at the side door to the house.

"I agree, Junior. It's time to go inside. I'm going to feed you guys and then take a really long hot shower."

Feeding the dogs didn't take long, and she fed the cats as well. She was glad that the other animals were fed in the mornings. She then showered the dirt off her body, wishing she had a shower massager. Especially when it took a great deal of effort to lift her legs to get out of the shower.

"Okay," she told no one in particular as she dried off with a fluffy blue towel, "maybe I overdid it. But at least it's done, right? A couple of aspirin and a good night's sleep will fix me right up."

She changed into a gray cropped tee-shirt and drawstring sweatshorts and made her way to the kitchen where she managed to eat a sandwich along with the aspirin.

In the living room, she cleared some space and sat down in Aunt Gracie's comfy overstuffed chair to watch some television, her feet propped up on an ottoman. An hour later, the program over and her eyelids drooping, Amelia decided to make an early night of it and go to bed.

Unfortunately, even though she told her legs to move, they didn't. Neither did her arms. None of her major muscle groups seemed to be functioning, she thought, an odd sense of impending doom enveloping her. What was she going to do? What if she had to go to the bathroom? How temporary was this condition? Sitting in this chair couldn't help matters, she told herself, and made a renewed, if futile, effort to get her body to cooperate. One leg managed to move a few inches, but the accompanying pain that started throbbing through her thigh made her stop and reconsider her options.

A knock on the door was followed by some serious barking by Junior and Fife, who left their cozy spots on the rug next to Amelia's chair to stand at the door and herald the coming of possible danger.

Unable to move, Amelia called out, "Who's there?"

The barking didn't stop, but she heard Adam's voice anyway. "It's me, Adam Larsen."

"Ssshh," she hissed at the dogs, who stopped barking. At least Junior did. Fife continued to growl and look menacingly at the door. Not wanting to let Adam know that she'd overdone her gardening project to the point of debilitating herself, she called out, "Uh, I'm about ready to go to bed, Adam. Could you come back tomorrow?"

But before she could finish the sentence, Fife started yipping frantically as the front door opened. Adam stepped into the foyer and looked around. When he saw Amelia parked in the chair, he closed the door and stepped through the archway into the living room. "I'm sorry. I couldn't hear you."

Fife attached himself to Adam's pant leg, but Adam just ignored him. He was apparently waiting for Amelia to say something.

"I, uh, nothing. What can I do for you?"

He seemed surprised, then frowned. "Nothing. I just stopped by to see how you were doing. I was surprised to see that you'd cleared the whole plot. Don't you think that's overdoing it? What's your hurry?"

Amelia would've shrugged if her shoulders had been in working order, but they weren't, so she just put on a completely false bubbly smile and said, "No hurry, but I figured, what the heck, I'm down here in the dirt, I might as well just get it done, you know? No time like the present and all that. What was it you said was the second step? Tilling? What exactly is involved in that?"

He took another step into the room, gently dragging Fife's tiny, growling body with him. "Tilling is turning the soil over to get it ready for planting." He stood looking at her for a moment, then said, "What's wrong?"

She still couldn't gesture, so she relied on her eyes and eyebrows, which she raised hoping for an expression of guile. "Nothing's wrong."

Adam's eyes weren't devoid of expression, either; and right now, they narrowed and gazed skeptically at her. "Right. So, everything's all right?"

Amelia nodded, glad that her neck muscles still functioned, albeit painfully. "Sure, why wouldn't everything be all right?"

He walked a few steps closer, which brought him next to her chair. Fife must have finally tired of his defensive tactics and let go of Adam's pant leg. The tiny dog backed away a few feet and stood watching his prey, occasionally growling as menacingly as he could. Junior just sat next to him, watching and wagging his tail, waving occasionally.

Adam crossed his arms over his solid chest and shrugged. "I don't know. Maybe because you didn't get up to answer the door and because you haven't moved an inch since I walked in."

Thinking fast under pressure had never been a strong suit of Amelia's, but she gave it her best shot. "Well, I'm sorry I didn't get to the door, but I think I fell asleep sitting here watching television and then you caught me off guard, I guess."

"Uh-huh."

He didn't look as if he believed her. In fact, instead of being a gentleman and at least pretending he believed her, he leaned forward and rested his hands on the arms of the chair, crowding her with his presence, with his scent and with his sexy blue eyes, which were now only inches from her flushed face.

"Wha—what are you doing?"

"Nothing," he said softly, his breath puffing gently against her face. "Why? Are you uncomfortable? Push me away if you are."

She tried to avoid his gaze, but couldn't. She could barely manage to blink. "I'm not uncomfortable," she lied. "Why would you think that?"

"You know, I've spent my life doing a lot of physical . . . labor."

And he had the body to show for it, she thought. Her focus then shifted to his lips and she couldn't help but think that no one should be allowed to be this sexy and this close to her without—

His lips settled on hers in midthought and Amelia sighed. His kiss was firm and confident and coaxing and demanding. Perfect. Lips that sexy just had to be this good at kissing. She wanted to pull him closer, but her arms wouldn't cooperate. He moved away a bit, and she tried to follow him, but an aching pain in her back wouldn't let her lean forward more than an inch.

Adam pulled away and looked at her solemnly. "You can't move a muscle, can you?"

She tried to muster another lie, but decided it just wasn't worth it. "Not one," she admitted.

"You didn't stretch like I told you, did you?"

Amelia tried to muster a withering glare. "I really don't need a lecture right now."

"Do you even have a clue as to what you need?"

She didn't think they were talking about the same thing. "I think that I need to get up and go to bed—to sleep," she added quickly. "So if you'd just lend me a bit of assistance, I'd appreciate it."

He shook his head and laughed at her. "Lady, you need more than sleep. Do you have any idea how stiff those muscles will be after eight hours of sleep? How long did it take for them to freeze up this time?"

Amelia looked up in horror. "An hour. Oh, my lord, Adam, what am I going to do? I'll be paralyzed!"

He waved his hands before her and said, "Whoa! Don't get hysterical. You just need a little liniment. I don't suppose you have any?"

She stared at him. "Liniment? Like they put on horses? What in the world would I do with liniment? No, I don't have any. Unless maybe Aunt Gracie had some. But I wouldn't know where to find it."

He held up a hand and took a step backward. "All right. I've got plenty. Is there a telephone in here somewhere?"

"It's over there on the little table next to the window."

Adam moved a few boxes and found the telephone and rapidly punched a number. Amelia was sure that all she needed to do was move around a bit and her body would loosen up. Of course, it would probably take several days of moving around.

"Harry? This is Adam. Can you or Joe bring over some liniment? I think it's in the downstairs bathroom."

"You know," Amelia began, "I think I'll be all right. I'll just soak in a really hot tub and I'll—"

"Sshh," Adam said, waving at her as he listened to Harry. Then, "Just bring it over, Harry."

He hung up the phone and came back over to her. "Soaking in hot water wouldn't hurt, but the liniment will be better. It'll penetrate into your muscles and heat them for hours. Trust me. It's the best thing to do."

"This stuff isn't like those menthol creams athletes use, is it?"

"Actually, it's a lot like that," he said, grinning. "So, not only does it relieve muscle aches—it clears your sinuses as well!"

Amelia rolled her eyes. "Great. A pitchman for an ad company."

"Okay, here's what we have to do: We have to get you up to your room, right?"

She looked wary, but acknowledged the fact. "Yes."

"Right. So, how should we go about this? I doubt you can make it on your own."

There was a gleam in his eye that Amelia didn't entirely trust. "Why don't you help me up and let's see if I can get myself into motion."

He shrugged and held out a hand. "Oh, I forgot," he said, and reached to grasp her wrists with his hands. He pulled gently upward and Amelia sucked in a lungful of surprised breath as her body protested the movement. "You okay?"

She nodded as she struggled to support her own weight. Her thigh and calf muscles seemed several inches shorter than her bones and the muscles in her back seemed to be pushing her forward. "I feel like I'm about 160 years old," she declared.

"Well, you don't look a day over 130," he assured her.

"Very funny," she huffed as she concentrated on remaining upright. "I bet you keep the cows in stitches."

Adam laughed and took a step backward, still holding

onto her wrists. "Nope. I'm a crops farmer, not a dairy farmer."

Each step was an experiment in pain, so letting the nearness of Adam Larsen distract her seemed like the best available option. "You don't have any cows? What kind of Wisconsin native are you?"

"Oh, I have a couple cows. Actually, they were my mother's. She thought she wanted to make her own butter and cheese once."

"Once?"

"Well, after a few months she realized what a lot of work went into getting that butter and cheese, so she gave it up. But by then she'd named the cows and didn't want to give *them* up."

Amelia stopped trying to move and stared up at Adam. "And after she passed away, you couldn't give them up either?"

"Well," he began, but quickly looked uncomfortable, so Amelia said, "I think that's very sweet. What are their names?"

"Clementine and Tallulah."

"I wonder if they'd like to come over and play with my cow. She has a tendency to wander. Maybe some companionship is what she's looking for."

"I think you're nuts. I also think that it's going to take you the rest of the night to get over to the stairs, much less up them."

Amelia didn't want to admit that he wasn't far from right. "Actually, it's getting easier. I just have to get loosened up a little."

"Amelia, I don't have that much time," he said and

suddenly swept her up into his arms. The protestations of the different parts of her body coalesced into one sound.

"Ow! Geez, that hurts. Put me down."

"I will," he promised, then proceeded into the foyer and up the stairs.

Under different circumstances, Amelia might've enjoyed this display of masculinity. But right now all she wanted was her soft bed. Liniment or no liniment.

Adam, with Amelia in his arms, was only on the third step when they heard a knock on the door behind them. Amelia sighed and said, "Come on in."

Her front door opened and both Harry and Joe stood on her porch gaping at them. Harry held up a tattered paper bag. "Here's that liniment you asked for."

Adam nodded. "Good. Thanks. Why don't you, uh . . ."

He looked around and finally said, "Just leave it there on the table, I guess."

Neither of the old men moved. They just stared at the sight of their boss holding Grace Appleberry's niece in his arms as he headed upstairs with her. Joe looked up speculatively and Harry followed suit.

"Whatcha need the, uh, liniment for, boss?" Harry inquired innocently. Something about the question sent Joe into a fit of snickering; then Harry couldn't contain himself, either.

Adam looked at Amelia and shook his head. "I think they need to get out more." To his farmhands he said, "All right, fellas, you've had your little laugh. Now leave the liniment, Harry, and go home."

Harry shrugged expansively. "No problem. I'm putting

it right here on the table. But I should warn you, that stuff is powerful, it can really, uh—"

"Sting," Joe chimed in.

"Right," Harry agreed. "Sting. Sting like the dickens."

This sent the two men into more snickering as they waved and backed out the door.

"Night, boss," Harry cooed.

"Night, Ms. Appleberry," Joe added.

"Good night, Harry. Good night, Joe," Amelia called out.

The door closed on their delighted faces and their laughter could still be heard as they made their way to their truck. Amelia looked at Adam. "I suppose that by tomorrow morning there won't be a person in town who hasn't heard about this."

Adam turned and headed back up the stairs. "A few, maybe. A shut-in or two. Whatever strangers are passing through town. But pretty much everybody else, yeah."

Amelia couldn't muster a lot of concern for a reputation she didn't have amongst people she didn't know, but it was a bit disconcerting to realize that everybody would have a preconceived notion about her before meeting her. "Well, I hope they won't treat me like the new town tramp."

Amelia could feel the rumbling of laughter in his chest. "I don't think you have anything to worry about. They'll probably just be curious about you."

They'd reached the top of the stairs and Adam paused, taking in the choices in doors. Amelia closed her eyes. "End of the hall."

He didn't say anything, just continued walking. When he got to the edge of her bed, he gently laid her on the brightly colored handmade quilt and straightened. Amelia lay still, wondering why her breathing had now gone south on her.

"I, um, I'm going to get that liniment," he said, and abruptly turned and left.

With a great deal of effort and not a little pain, Amelia managed to wrestle a pillow under her head and then fell back on it. How she would manage rubbing liniment on herself, especially her back, she didn't know. And she wasn't about to ask Adam to do it. Although the thought of his hands rubbing her skin . . . with liniment?

"Get a grip, Amelia," she muttered to herself.

Two of the three sisters appeared from under the bed and sprang up next to her.

"Olga. Masha. Where's Irina?" A muffled meow came from under the bed. "All right," Amelia said. "I just wanted to make sure you were okay."

Adam reappeared at the door with the large bottle of cloudy-looking liniment in his hand and Junior at his heels. They heard a tiny yip that turned into pathetic yowl.

"Fife can't climb the stairs," Amelia explained as she absently stroked Olga's fur. "And he doesn't like to be left alone."

"I hope you don't expect me to go get him," Adam said.

"No, of course not," she denied, then turned to look at Junior. "Junior? Go get Fife."

The brown-and-white dog cocked his head at her, then turned and trotted away, his tail waving like a flag behind him.

Adam shook his head and held up the bottle of liniment. "Now this may smell bad, but it'll make you feel better."

Amelia didn't like the sound of that. "Just how bad does it smell? I mean, am I going to barf or something?"

"No," he insisted, "it's just strong. That menthol, you know."

She still wasn't convinced this was such a good idea; but before she could say so, Junior reappeared in the doorway, holding Fife by the scrap of his collar. The Chihuahua puppy appeared to be suffering the indignity of it all when he saw Adam and started growling.

Adam stared at the spectacle. "I don't believe it. He actually went and got Fife."

Amelia didn't know why he should sound so surprised. "Of course, he did. I told him to." She turned to the dogs and said, "Put Fife down, Junior."

Which he did. Fife promptly launched a renewed attack on Adam's pant leg while Junior sat down, wagging his tail and enjoying the show. Olga and Masha crept to the edge of the bed and looked intently at Fife. Another meow came from Irina under the bed as she poked her head out to see what the fuss was about.

Choosing to ignore the animal circus, Adam unscrewed the cap on the liniment and approached Amelia. "You might as well get used to this smell, because it'll be with you for a while."

He waved it in front of her nose and Amelia thought her eyebrows got singed. It was so far beyond the drugstore variety mentholated rubbing creams in sheer intensity of odor that she felt her sinuses rebelling.

Fife whined and let go of Adam's pant leg, then ran and stood behind Junior, who raised his nose, whined, and suddenly turned and ran out of the room, Fife close on his heels. The three sisters were just a few streaks of yowling, mottled colored fur as they, too, made a hasty exit.

"Well," Adam reasoned, "now I know how to get you alone."

Amelia laughed. "Yes, anything that foul smelling is sure to clear any room of sentient beings. At least, any sentient beings that are mobile."

"Once you get used to it," Adam assured her, "you'll hardly notice it."

"And what about anybody unlucky enough to be down-wind of me?"

"They're on their own. Now, turn over."

She gaped at him. "I—what?"

"I said, turn over." He waggled the bottle of liniment at her. "So I can rub this on you."

Amelia's throat suddenly became drier than the Mojave as she struggled to speak. "I . . . that is . . . do you really think that's necessary? I mean, maybe you should just leave it and I'll—"

"You'll what?" Adam asked. "You'll be able to get this on your back and shoulders? Can you even sit up right now?"

Determination flared in her and she jerked herself into a sitting position. "Oooowwww!"

"You're rather stubborn, aren't you?"

She shot him the most withering glare she could muster under the circumstances. "Ha, ha."

"Turn over. I promise that I won't take liberties with your admittedly provocative body."

"I don't have a provocative body," she denied, nevertheless pleased that he'd said she did.

"It's all a matter of perspective, Amelia. And from my perspective . . . oh, just turn over."

She was without recourse, she thought. Of course, she could insist and he would, most likely, do as she requested.

She turned over, trying not to groan. And waited. All she could think about was the brief kiss they had shared downstairs. Why had he done that? To prove a point? To tease her? And had he forgotten about it as soon as it was over or was he thinking about it right now?

"This might burn a little," he said. "Especially since you seem to have such . . . delicate skin. Let me know if it really hurts and I'll dilute it."

"All right," she agreed, bracing herself more for the touch of his hands on her skin than the damned liniment.

That first touch, nevertheless, caused her to suck in a lungful of air on a hiss. It burned, but didn't hurt. The only thing she could liken it to was putting peroxide on a cut.

"You okay?" Adam asked as he began to massage the stuff into the muscle of her right calf.

"Um, yeah, I guess," she answered between sucking breaths. "It's not too bad."

"See? And it'll start to make you feel better any second now."

She didn't really care about the goop he was massaging her with, just that he was moving his hands up and down her leg, kneading the sore muscles and then smoothing gently along her skin. It felt wonderful. Maybe a little too wonderful. Maybe a little too much burning of another type altogether.

He started on the other leg and Amelia realized that she really did feel better. The heat from the liniment seeped into the soreness and relieved it somewhat. Enough that she could flex her muscles without their throbbing in protest. Her eyes closed as she enjoyed the massage and the gradual easing of her aches.

When his fingers reached the top of her thigh and continued up under her shorts, her eyes popped open and she felt her body tense. "Hey, what—"

"Don't get all indignant," he said quickly, continuing to massage her derriere under her shorts. "Is this a muscle or not?"

"That's not the—"

"It is. It's the gluteus maximus."

"I know that," she told him. "But—"

"But nothing. Unless this muscle miraculously escaped the abuse you heaped upon the rest of your body."

When he put it that way it sounded almost clinical, she reasoned. However, to her way of thinking, it was anything but clinical. It was downright sexual. And since she couldn't see his face, she couldn't gauge what he might really think about it.

His hands moved on to her back as he pushed her top up to begin work on the muscles of her back.

"I don't suppose you'd like to take your shirt off?"

Amelia didn't answer him.

"I'll take that as a *no*," he said, laughing softly.

He continued massaging the liniment into her back and up to her shoulders and neck under the shirt. It really did feel wonderfully warm and soothing. And she hardly even noticed the smell anymore. Okay, she did, but it wasn't as overpowering.

This had to be one of the strangest experiences of her life. She really didn't know Adam Larsen well enough to allow him this sort of intimate contact, but something about him made her trust him.

He was good with his hands, she thought fuzzily as those same hands slid down the sides of her waist and back up.

Her arms were then pulled and kneaded, but she didn't care. Everything he did now felt marvelous. Everywhere he touched tingled and felt warm. She wasn't entirely sure that that was due only to the liniment. No, it was more than that. It was . . .

FOUR

It took a few minutes for Adam to realize that Amelia had fallen asleep. His hands paused, but a sleepy murmur of protest from Amelia prompted him to continue.

He looked down at her prone, sleeping body and muttered, "Well, Larsen, you've got the most desirable woman you've met in years half naked on her bed. Unfortunately, she's unconscious and reeking of liniment."

From the hallway, he heard a small whine and turned to see the two dogs and three cats just outside the door.

"Shhh," he warned them. "Amelia's asleep."

He walked out into the hallway and the animals fled before the scent still lingering on his hands. "All right, all right," he said quietly, "I'll wash it off."

He found the bathroom two doors down and went in to wash his hands. It took a lot of soap and water, but he finally thought he was more or less rid of the menthol odor.

The animals were gathered in the hallway again and they didn't run from him this time, so he stood and looked at them. "Well, guys, I have to tell you, your mistress is missing a few of the crucial screws that keep the wheels on her wagon."

Fife growled at him.

"I didn't mean that she isn't nice. She is nice. Very nice. And pretty. And sweet. And sexy . . ."

One of the cats began doing a figure eight between his legs and he reached down absently to stroke her fur, then knelt on one knee as the others crept closer, hoping for a little attention.

"But you have to understand," he continued. "She really doesn't belong here. I mean, look what she did to herself today."

Junior nudged Adam's free hand and got a few ear scratches as a reward. "I mean, sure, I admire her determination and spunk, and I can appreciate that she's trying to find herself and all . . . but why here? Why now? And why can't she find herself in town? Why does it have to be on this piece of land?"

The other cats had joined in the petting fest, but Fife held back, standing stiff legged by the opposite wall, growling as deeply as he could.

"Okay," Adam nodded, looking at the little dog as if he'd just caught him red-handed. "I want the land. But it's not like I want to cheat her out of it. I'm willing to pay fair market value for it. No, *more* than market value. But she's too stubborn to listen to reason.

He sank down on the floor of the hallway, the cats and Junior either lying on his legs or leaning against him. He looked down the hall at Amelia's open bedroom door. His hands still held the memory of what her skin felt like—healthy and firm, yet soft. He shouldn't have let his hands stray under her shorts, but he couldn't say he was sorry. He'd wanted to strip her dinky little shorts and top off and make love to her right then and there.

"But gentlemen don't take advantage of ladies who are trusting them to help and not . . ."

He still wanted to, he admitted to himself. Nothing wrong with that. And maybe when she recovered she'd want to as well.

"Can't hurt to ask, now, can it?"

Fife actually yipped at him and the force of it propelled the little dog into a skid that ended when he slid into the side of Adam's booted foot. There was barely an impact, so Fife wasn't hurt; but his dignity suffered mightily, so he growled and attacked the offending boot.

"Okay, maybe I shouldn't just ask. Some women find that too rude. And I think Amelia might be one of them."

The cats purred and Junior pushed at his hand when he stopped scratching his ears. Fife continued to think he was making mincemeat out of the boot. Adam reasoned to them, "I don't want her to think that I'm only after the land. I am, but I wouldn't sleep with her to get it. I least I hope I wouldn't. I would like to sleep with her, though. The sleep part being optional. Besides, it's not like she doesn't know that I want the land. She knew that before we met."

Amelia's dogs and cats weren't sharing their opinions with Adam, except for Fife, who made it pretty clear that he didn't like him the least little bit. "Maybe I should give her some time," he concluded. "Sooner or later she'll realize that she isn't a farmer. Probably when she wakes up tomorrow morning, if she hasn't already."

He chuckled to himself, remembering how he'd kissed her when she couldn't push him away. "I probably shouldn't have done that, either," he said. Then he grinned. "She didn't have to kiss me back, though, did she?"

The cats just purred and Junior snuggled into his side. Fife ceased his attack on the boot and sneezed, then stalked away, still growling.

Amelia wasn't sure exactly what woke her the next morning. It could have been the bright sunshine peeking around the edges of the drawn shades in her room. Shades she didn't remember pulling. Or was it the drone of farm equipment being used by one of her neighbors?

Usually, it was one of the animals who woke her. But, as she opened her eyes and gazed blearily around, not one of them was in sight. And what was that vile smell? It took her a moment to realize that it was she. Sniffing a whiff of the vile-smelling ointment that still clung to her skin, she wrinkled her nose. She didn't blame any living creature for avoiding her.

Suddenly, her eyes popped opened as she remembered just how she had come to be so aromatic. She felt her cheeks flush as she remembered Adam's hands moving over her skin. She covered her eyes with her hands and moaned. "I fell asleep!"

She rolled over and felt her sore muscles protest. But the pain was nothing in comparison to how she'd been feeling last night. Gingerly, she stretched her legs, grateful that they moved when she told them to without cramping. At least now she could get around on her own.

Unlike last night when Adam had had to carry her up the stairs. Under different circumstances she might have enjoyed the whole night. "Not that there weren't enjoyable parts of the evening," she mumbled to herself.

The unexpected kiss had been nice. It would have been better if she'd been able to touch him. But what if he'd only done it as a joke? To goad her into admitting that she'd overworked herself? It hadn't felt like an impersonal, proving-a-point kind of kiss, but what did she know?

"I know that he now knows my butt better than he should," she muttered as she sat up slowly and slid her legs over the edge of the bed. When her feet met the floor, she took a deep breath and stood up.

When she didn't fall down again, she counted it as a major victory. She had to give the smelly liniment credit; it worked wonders. Or had it been the massage technique of Adam Larsen?

Amelia made her way into the hallway toward the bathroom and found Irina and Olga sitting at the top of the stairs, eyeing her.

"Hello, girls. How are you?"

They started toward her, then stopped, hissed, and fled down the stairs.

"I guess I need to take a shower," she grimaced ruefully.

Half an hour later, after a hot shower refreshed her and reduced her aching muscles to a minor annoyance, Amelia headed down the stairs in search of some serious breakfast.

She could still hear the drone of that farm equipment. It must be one of Adam's farmhands working on a field nearby. Something made her stop as she walked into the kitchen. Something about that machine noise.

It was too loud. It seemed too close. She went to the window and leaned forward, looking first ahead, then to the left. There, at the edge of her recently cleared garden plot stood an old man. In her garden, walking behind a machine that seemed to be chewing up the soil as it went over it, was another old man.

"What are they doing?" she said aloud. She heard a soft snort and looked down to find Junior prancing at her feet. "Hey, you." She leaned down to pet him. "Decided that I'm safe enough to smell again?"

The dog woofed happily and ran to the side door.

"You need to go out? Well, so do I. I have to find out why two elderly gentlemen are tilling my garden."

Junior apparently wasn't really concerned about Amelia's problems and just stood with his nose at the crack of the door until Amelia opened it for him. Just then Fife appeared in the doorway to the kitchen and yipped. Amelia waited as he shook his way over to the door and delicately picked his way outside. Just as she was about to step outside, a plastic cake cover fell off the top of the refrigerator. Amelia jumped as it hit the floor and looked up. "God, Zilla! You scared the bejeezus out of me." The iguana peered at her from atop the refrigerator.

"You want to go outside for a while? Well, come on."

She picked up the iguana and cradled her in the crook of her arm as she left the house. Junior and Fife were making sure all the trees and shrubbery were still in place as Amelia walked outside; then they fell into step behind her.

She headed straight for the garden to question the old men. They seemed to be having some sort of argument as she approached. At least, the one standing at the edge of the garden was trying to argue with the other one, who either couldn't hear over the noise of the tiller or pretended he couldn't hear.

She then realized that they were the same men who had brought the liniment last night. Last night. She could remember being held in Adam's strong arms as two old men goggled at them in disbelief. They probably thought she was a hussy, or something. She hadn't gotten a really good look at them as they'd hovered on her doorstep, but she definitely recognized the one yelling as Harry. The one who'd actually come inside and left the liniment.

Now, why had Adam sent two of his farmhands over here to do work that Amelia had said she wanted to do herself? Before she could come up with an answer, they saw her. The one with the tiller turned the machine off after finishing the last pass and walked through the soft, plowed dirt to stand next to his coworker. Both had a weather-beaten, grizzled look that spoke of years spent in the sun and cold.

The one who'd been tilling tipped his hat with the tractor logo on it and, after casting a wary eye at Zilla, cleared his throat. "Uh, hello, ma'am. I'm Joe, and this here is Harry," he said, jerking a thumb at his companion. "We work for the Larsens."

Fife must have suddenly realized that the men were strangers and bolted forward, yipping and yapping for all he was worth, circling the two men until he got into the dirt of the garden, then backing up and going the other way. Joe and Harry looked down at the tiny dog and then looked back at each other, shaking their heads.

Amelia nodded. "I see." But she really didn't. "And why did Mr. Larsen send you gentlemen over here?"

They preened at being called *gentlemen,* but Amelia wondered what justification Adam would have for going against her express wishes regarding the preparation of the plot for her garden.

Neither said anything for a moment as they stood and looked at her. And Zilla. Then Harry nudged Joe. Joe looked annoyed. "What?" he questioned, then turned to Harry, who gestured to Amelia. Joe suddenly seemed to get something straight in his mind. "Right. I mean, Mr. Adam didn't send us. We decided that since he was giving you the seeds as a . . . uhh"—he frowned—"ah . . . er . . ."

Harry rolled his eyes. "Good gravy you are getting old. A housewarming present."

Joe bristled. "I was about to say that. And since you're older'n me, I'd put the kibosh on that talk about me being old."

"Dadgum it, get on with it, already," Harry yelled.

Amelia tried to keep her expression pleasant as she waited for the two men to finish, but it was difficult. She wanted to laugh and hug them both. But they probably wouldn't have understood.

Joe cleared his throat. "Well, we figured we'd give you something, too. And since you were going to plant the seeds, we figured we would help out by getting it ready."

"The garden," Harry clarified.

Joe gave Harry a look of disgust. "Of course, the garden, what else? She ain't dumb; she can see that it's the garden."

They looked about to start another argument, so Amelia quickly said, "Adam didn't send you?"

They shook their heads. Harry shifted from one foot

to the other and said, "You see, we heard Mr. Adam talking about how you wanted to do the garden just like Miz Grace done it."

Amelia was surprised that Adam had been talking about her. "Really? Well, that's true. That's why I cleared out all the weeds and old plants myself yesterday."

Joe nodded. "Yep, Miz Grace was stubborn that way, too. Must be something about being a Appleberry woman."

Harry rolled his eyes. "That's right, Joe, insult her right to her face. She won't mind much."

"I didn't insult nobody," Joe denied.

Fife tired of his perimeter march and backed up to growl and yap. Amelia turned her attention briefly to the Chihuahua. "Fife, sit down and stop growling at the nice gentlemen," she commanded.

The little dog sat down and actually did stop growling. Instead, he sort of sneered at them, lifting his lip and showing them his tiny teeth. Joe gaped at Fife. "Did you see that?"

Harry shrugged. "So what?"

"I take it you two knew my Aunt Gracie?"

"Oh, sure," Joe said expansively.

"Yep," Harry added. "She was a crusty old bird. We used to help her out now and again, even though she acted like we did everything wrong."

"Speak for yourself," Joe said. "Me and Miz Grace usually got along fine."

Harry took exception. "She liked me just as much as she liked you—and prob'ly more. Besides," he turned to tell Amelia, "she couldn't take care of this place by herself."

" 'Course, she'd give you a tongue-lashing if she ever heard you saying that," Harry put in.

Amelia didn't know why she should be surprised. Someone had to have helped an elderly woman take care of twenty acres of land and the various animals and buildings that went along with it. Still, the thought of these two missing members of the over-the-hill gang with her aunt was strange.

"I see," she finally said. "But I was under the impression that Aunt Gracie was a stickler for doing the garden herself without . . . um . . . assistance from modern machinery."

Joe and Harry looked like a couple of kids caught in a lie. "Well, uh," Joe stammered, and then he looked at Harry.

Harry cleared his throat, adjusted his hat, and said, "Well, Miz Amelia, I'll tell you something. Miz Grace liked to think she didn't have much use for machinery, but when she went to town after clearing her plot—"

"Which she'd do over a week or so," Joe interrupted, looking at Amelia pointedly. "Not in one day."

Harry scowled at Joe. "Now, don't she know that was a dumb thing to do? Anybody needing that liniment and needing to be carried up the stairs like that?"

Amelia refused to feel embarrassed. "So, you know what happened?"

Joe nodded. "Sure. Mr. Adam set us straight this morning. Didn't want us to get the wrong idea about you. And him."

"Anyhow," Harry said loudly, "Miz Grace would go into town and me and Joe would always come over and till her garden for her."

Joe beamed. "That's right. She'd stomp around and yell and complain about how a body couldn't turn their back for a minute in this county, but we knew she sure did appreciate it."

He and Harry then laughed and shook their heads. After a minute, Harry sighed. "So. We figured we'd do the same for you. Only we didn't know when you might be going into town."

"So we thought we'd just do it as a . . . whatchacallit," Joe said, reaching for the word. Harry threw up his hands.

"A housewarming present, you idjit!"

"Well, it ain't like it's for her house, now is it?" Joe claimed. "Ought to be called a garden-warming present."

Harry started to take exception to that, so Amelia quickly said, "Well, I think it's a lovely present, and I thank both of you. It was rather dumb of me to overdo it yesterday, and what you've done will save me a lot of aches and pains. It was very sweet of you."

They both beamed and Amelia thought she might have to adopt the both of them.

"Well, Miz Amelia," Harry said after a moment, "I guess we'd better be getting on back. If you ever need any advice about farming, don't be shy about asking us."

After stepping around the still sneering Fife, they loaded the tiller into the bed of Harry's dilapidated truck and left, Joe waving from the passenger window.

Amelia waved back and felt a twinge in her shoulder. She looked at the freshly turned soil and heaved a sigh of relief. This was absolutely the best garden-warming present she'd ever received.

* * *

The truck trundled to the road and slowed. Harry pulled over to the side, and Joe looked over at him in surprise.

"Something wrong?"

Harry shook his head. "Naw. I was just thinking."

Joe cackled, "Always a first time for everything."

"Shut up," Harry shot back. "I'm serious."

"About what?"

Harry jerked a thumb back toward Amelia's place. "Whaddya think of the new Miz Appleberry?"

Joe shrugged. "I guess she's okay. Seems nice enough. I don't know about that lizard, though. Strikes me as a tetch strange." He then grinned. "Boss had his hands full with her last night, if you know what I mean."

"Yeah, I do. Sure would solve a lot of problems if those two got together, dontcha think?"

Joe frowned. "What problems?"

Harry shoved the truck into drive and pulled back onto the road. "You are dumber'n a boxa rocks."

"What? All I said was what problems?"

Harry nodded. "Exactly. Anyhow, what does Mr. Adam want more'n anything right now?" Before Joe could take a guess, he continued. "The Appleberry land. And who owns the Appleberry land?"

Joe was quicker with this one. "Amelia Appleberry!"

"Score one for your side. Now, wouldn't it be just fine if those two nice young people got together and—"

"And Mr. Adam wouldn't have to pay for the land at all," Joe surmised. "He could marry it, instead." He mulled this over. "I don't know. Might be easier in the long run to just pay her for it."

Harry shook his head. "You ain't much of a romantic, are you, Joe?"

"All's I'm saying is that the rest of your life is a pretty steep price for twenty acres of land."

Harry shook his head and snorted in disgust.

Adam saw the truck pull up in the gravel parking area near the first barn and strode toward it. Harry and Joe took their time getting out of the truck, then, seeing Adam waiting, ambled over.

"You looking for us, Mr. Adam?"

"Just wondered where you'd got off to," Adam said. He knew they'd gone over to Amelia's, but he wasn't going to grill them about it, even if they had taken off in the middle of the morning on a workday.

Joe scratched his throat. "Well, we went over to rototill that garden Miz Appleberry is setting up."

Adam nodded, relieved that Amelia wouldn't be doing any more of the physically demanding labor a garden that size demanded. Of course, if she weren't so determined to be all things to gardening overnight, she wouldn't have practically incapacitated herself in one day.

"She ask you to do that?"

Harry shook his head. "Naw. But we used to do the same thing—kind of on the sly—for her aunt."

"So, we figured we'd keep up the tradition," Joe finished. " 'Course, it used to make Miz Grace hopping mad. Kinda used to like watching her get all riled up."

Adam nodded. "Uh-huh. And how did Amelia react when she saw what you'd done?"

Harry stuck his hands on his hips and seemed to consider this. "Well, I'm thinking she liked it. She wuddn't hopping up and down with joy, but she looked like she was glad it was all done. Ain't that right, Joe?"

"I guess that's about right. Actually she seemed kinda off a little. You know, like somebody'd whacked her on the head with something hard."

Harry gaped at Joe. "She seemed no such thing!"

"At first, she did," Joe insisted. "Came out of that house with her dogs . . . and that lizard thing. It was pretty weird if you ask me. And she smiles like there ain't nothing strange about it."

Adam tried not to laugh. "Yeah, she has a thing about animals. So, the garden's ready for planting?"

Harry nodded. "Yep. Gotta be fertilized, of course. And raked and all, but yep, ready."

"Okay. Well, that was real nice of you two to do that for her."

"Aw, we didn't mind," Joe said. "Did we, Harry?"

"Not a bit."

"Well, I've got to get back to replacing that old irrigation pipe. You two gonna work on that fencing?"

"Yep, that's it," Harry promised.

Joe shot him with his finger. "Yes, sir."

Adam nodded and headed for his truck. He started for the road that would take him to the farther reaches of his farm. He glanced in the rearview mirror and saw Joe and Harry standing where he'd left them, deep in conversation.

"They're up to something," he muttered. Then he looked to the east and caught sight of the top of the buildings of the Appleberry place. Maybe he should stop over there later today and see if Amelia needed any help planting those seeds he gave her.

At a little past five, Adam emerged from the bathroom freshly showered and shaved and met Jason in the hallway. There was no way to avoid the inevitable, so he resigned himself to it.

"My, my," Jason exclaimed, "aren't you pretty? And why, if I may be allowed to ask, are you not only inside at this hour but looking"—he sniffed the air—"and smelling like a man with a hot date?"

"I just decided to take a shower a little earlier than usual, all right?" He looked down at his clean blue jeans and polo shirt. He was not dressed up.

Jason laughed. "Doesn't matter to me. I don't have to smell you. So, where're you going? No wait," he interrupted himself. "Let me guess. You're going to visit that apparently plain woman who's moved in next door. Planning on seducing the land out from under her?"

Adam scowled. "No, I don't." He didn't like how Jason put it. Like he was up to something underhanded and manipulative. "I'm just going over to talk to the woman, and I didn't think I should do it covered in dirt and grime."

Jason bowed mockingly. "Gentlemanly of you, I'm sure."

Adam glared at him. "And what are *you* doing home early?"

"Same as you, big brother, same as you. Got to get myself ready for a date with a beautiful woman."

Adam nodded and started down the stairs, then turned. "I'm not going on a date."

"Whatever you say."

He stomped down the stairs, annoyed with himself that he'd let his brother's teasing get to him. He didn't normally rise so easily to the bait. It was Amelia, he thought. She made him think and do things he never did.

He grabbed a relatively clean hat off the rack near the back door and plopped it on his head. He'd almost made it to his truck when he saw Joe and Harry emerge from the barn. They had to have seen him, because they fairly hopscotched over to where he stood next to the truck.

"So, going over to see the new Miz Appleberry?"

Adam wondered what it might be like to be a private person. "Yes, I am. I thought I'd see how she's doing and if she needs any help or advice on how to plant the seeds."

Joe looked up at the still-bright sky. "Well, it's almost too late to be planting seeds. Shoulda started the seeds a few weeks ago so they'd be started by now."

Harry agreed. "Almost the end of May now."

"I know that," Adam told them. "But since she only got here a few days ago, there isn't much I can do about that, now, is there?"

Harry shrugged. "You never know. Might have a longer summer than normal. Might give her that extra couple weeks of summer growing."

Joe contemplated this. "Might."

Adam shook his head. "That's a good point, fellas."

"Hmmm, you look like you're ready to go to church," Joe said.

Adam ignored him and got into the truck. Harry and

Joe stood grinning at him. "Have a good time," Harry called out as the truck pulled away. The last thing Adam saw before pulling onto the road was a glimpse of Joe and Harry in the rearview, waving.

He didn't know what he'd done to deserve it all, but it must have been something pretty heinous. He could have let himself dwell longer on his family and employees and their buttinsky attitudes, but he pulled into the drive leading to the Appleberry place and promptly shut them all out.

He pulled up in front of the house next to another truck. He recognized it as Eddie O'Brien's. What would Eddie be doing here? He looked around, but didn't see Amelia near the garden or the barn. He knocked on the door, but got no response. Then he thought he heard voices and headed around back.

He rounded the corner of the house to find Amelia sitting on the ground, playing with a puppy. Off to the side stood Maggie O'Brien and her son Matt. Well, that explained the truck, he thought. He heard a bark and saw Amelia's dog Junior bounding around near the puppy, who was pulling at something Amelia had.

"I think Leo's just a little bored, Mrs. O'Brien," Amelia said, waggling a hunk of rope at the puppy.

"Call me *Maggie*. I can appreciate that he's bored," she said with a sigh, "but I don't appreciate that my shoes and the TV remote control and anything else that happens to be within reach gets chewed up.

Amelia nodded and looked from the puppy to the little boy who stood anxiously nearby. "Well, I don't think you should give up on him just yet. When does school get out for the summer?"

"Not for another two weeks," Matt said glumly.

"Okay. How about this—you bring Leo over here while you're at school and he can play with Junior and Junior will show him that he shouldn't chew people things. Then, after school you can pick him up and take him home and watch him to make sure he's behaving himself. How's that?"

Matt looked hopefully to his mother, who shrugged. "I suppose that would be all right. Do you really think you can stop him from chewing everything?"

By now Matt was jumping up and down and hugging Leo. Amelia laughed and then nodded to Maggie. "I think so. Most puppies like to chew. It's just a matter of getting their energy refocused. Give them chew toys. Play with them a lot to deal with their excess energy. Junior can handle that."

"What'll it cost?"

Amelia's hand hit her chest, then waved vigorously. "Don't worry about that. What's one more dog? It would be my pleasure."

"Well, okay. Matt, will you remember to bring some food with you when you bring Leo over?"

Matt nodded happily to his mother. "Sure.

"All right then," Maggie agreed. "This just sounds kind of weird, you know?"

Amelia shrugged. "Maybe. But if it works, what's the difference?"

"I guess you're right about that. Well, come on, Matt. We have to get home and get dinner ready."

As they said their good-byes, Adam heard a familiar growl and looked down just in time to see Fife launch his attack on Adam's pant leg. He was about to disentangle the scrappy dog when the others saw him.

"Hi, Adam," Amelia called. "Fife, leave Adam alone. He's not going to hurt us."

The Chihuahua let go—somewhat reluctantly, Adam thought—and backed up, lifting his lip every once in a while.

The O'Briens both found this display very humorous. Especially Maggie, who'd gone to high school with Adam. "Better watch out, Adam," she called as she and Matt and Leo got into the truck. "Amelia's guard dog is pretty vicious."

Adam smiled and hoped it didn't look fake. "Yeah, I noticed."

They all waved as the truck pulled away; then Amelia turned back to Adam. "Well, hello again. What brings you back? Did you come to look for your trunk? I still haven't seen it. I'm beginning to wonder if it really exists."

He shook his head. "No, I'm not really concerned about the trunk. I just finished up at my place and thought I'd come over and see if you were having any trouble planting."

Amelia's happy expression slipped a bit. "Well, actually, I haven't started it yet."

"Really?" He was surprised. After the way she'd tackled clearing the plot, he'd figured she'd have had the garden half planted by now.

"Well, after I fed the livestock and let them out for some exercise, I spent some time in the house, straightening and putting things away, and then I cleaned out the stalls in the barn, and then I lost the cow and had to go get her, and then Matt and Maggie O'Brien came over and—"

"And you've been busy."

She sighed loudly. "Yes. But that's probably not the only reason. I've been reading my gardening book, and I still have to fertilize and I'm not sure how and—"

Adam laughed and Amelia stopped and stared at him, wide-eyed. "What?"

He pointed to the barn. "Amelia, you have a barn full of fertilizer."

She paused as she gazed at the barn. "My gosh, I do, don't I? But the book said that real, um, cow, um, fertilizer would probably be full of the weeds that the cow had eaten and that then my garden would be full of those weeds."

Adam was impressed by her grasp of those principles. "Well, yes, that's true. But since the cow in question is eating weeds that grow right here, then you'd likely get those weeds anyway.

She nodded. "Right. So, what do I do? Just shovel it into the garden plot?"

"Pretty much. You rake the soil and then form the rows for the seeds, then mix the fertilizer into the soil, then plant the seeds."

She tilted her head to one side as she considered his words. "That doesn't sound so difficult."

She didn't really sound convinced, so he said, "It's a concept that's been around for thousands of years. It can be hard physically, but the principle is a basic one."

"Okay, then," she said with a bit more confidence. "I'll get started on it."

With that, she turned toward the gardening shed. Adam

stared after her. "I didn't mean right now," he said to empty space.

Fife growled at him.

Adam surprised Amelia by staying and offering to help her with the garden. She'd returned from the shed with a rake and a hoe and found him contemplating her garden. Actually, the patch of dirt where her garden would soon be.

"You don't have to do that," she said, taking in his clean clothes and fresh-from-a-shower scent that had her sidling closer just to smell him. "You probably have things to do," she said lamely. "People to see."

He quirked an eyebrow at her and gave her a lopsided grin. "Actually, I hadn't really planned anything past coming over here and seeing if you needed help." He paused, then said, "Unless you'd rather do it all yourself."

Amelia shook her head. "I've decided that mankind was put here to help each other and those who try to do everything themselves are punished for it. Witness my own catastrophe of yesterday."

The expression in his eyes told her that he remembered every bit of yesterday just fine. She felt herself start to flush and turned away, almost tripping over the rake.

Mercifully, Adam merely replied. "I'd just as soon help you out a bit. But don't let it get around town that I'm moonlighting, okay?"

Amelia laughed and nodded, then looked up at him. "I wanted to thank you . . . for talking to Joe and Harry. I mean, for setting them straight about what happened last night."

Something flared in his blue eyes and his smile became almost smug. "You're welcome. But I didn't tell them what really happened, of course."

"What do you mean, 'what really happened'? Nothing happened," she protested, thinking wildly. Had something happened? No, definitely not. She could remember every touch, every sensation of his hands on her body. She'd remember if there had been anything else. Except that she'd fallen asleep.

"Oh, I know," he said calmly. A bit too calmly for Amelia. "Why don't we go and load up a wheelbarrow with manure and get started?"

FIVE

They raked and hoed and measured distances between rows and mixed the several-days-old manure into the soil. Amelia decided it was a stinky, icky job. But after about two-and-a-half hours, it was almost done. The sun was setting, and the Wisconsin sky was turning various shades of orange and lavender and pink. She was tired, but it wasn't a debilitating tired. It was more of a satisfying tired.

Adam stood on the grass, not far from the dwindled pile of manure they'd used to fertilize the soil. They'd dumped several wheelbarrows full of the cow's contribution next to the garden and then shoveled it and spread it accordingly. Amelia had to admit that the smell wasn't nearly as bad as she expected. Something about letting it dry for a day or three, Adam had told her. Not that it was pleasant now, but at least she wasn't ready to gag.

"Imagine doing this over hundreds of acres," Adam told her.

"I couldn't possibly," she said as she made her last little seed gutter in a ridge of soil. "I now know why people used to have shorter life spans. They worked themselves to death trying to grow their own food."

Adam laughed. "Don't be silly. They were serfs, and the gentlemen farmers worked them to death."

Amelia finished her row and walked over to where Adam stood on the grass. "Is that what you are? A gentleman farmer?"

"Sure," he said, leaning on his rake. "Can't you tell just by looking at me?"

"Well, I know you're a gentleman," Amelia said calmly.

His self-mocking expression slipped a bit when he realized she wasn't really joking. "You do? And how do you know that?"

She probably shouldn't have said anything, but it was too late now. So she took a deep breath and said, "Because of the way you treated me last night. You tried to warn me not to do too much, but I wouldn't listen and then you had to rescue me from myself. I'm sorry I fell asleep. I would have thanked you."

He rocked the rake back and forth, then looked down at her. "You're welcome. Although, I have to admit that it wasn't just a medical mission for me."

Did he mean what she thought he meant? "It wasn't?"

He shook his head. "Nope. I confess. I derived a certain amount of pleasure from last night."

Amelia floundered. Finally, "I can't imagine that. I mean, I was reeking of that liniment and I was rude and suspicious."

Adam laughed. "You had a right to be suspicious. You have a beautiful body and I liked touching it last night. The liniment was necessary, but it also gave me a chance to touch you, and I enjoyed it."

"Oh. Well, then," she managed, despite a sudden complete lack of moisture in her mouth.

He reached out and brushed a long strand of brown hair away from her face, but then his fingers lingered at her cheek. "It wasn't fair of me to kiss you the way I did last night, either," he said softly, his fingers brushing over her cheek to her jaw.

Amelia felt her heart slamming into her ribs and was glad he couldn't see it until his thumb brushed her throat and she knew he could feel her pulse racing. After a moment she managed, "Why wasn't it fair?"

"Because you weren't in a position to push me away and say no."

"Why would I do that?"

He leaned forward, and then he was kissing her and Amelia was so glad that she now had the use of her arms. She wrapped them around his waist and strained toward him, deepening the kiss.

The rake fell to the ground with a soft thud as his hands slid around her waist and pulled her closer. Amelia's hands crept up the sinewy muscles of his arms to his shoulders until her fingers brushed against the hair at the back of his neck.

His tongue teased her lips and they parted eagerly. They tasted and probed and explored with their lips and tongues, and Amelia felt her skin burning wherever she touched Adam. Her arms, her legs, her chest, her belly. Deep within her, desire curled and grew and she pushed closer to him, wanting to feel the hardness of his body against her softness.

She didn't realize he'd tugged her shirt from the waist of her shorts until she felt his warm hands skimming over the skin of her waist and ribcage, then moving slowly up to capture her breasts. He seemed to know exactly how to touch her and where. Every nerve ending in her body vibrated in tune with each caress.

Amelia sagged against him, her knees totally unreliable. Adam's lips left hers and trailed across her cheek to her ear and then to her neck. Each new assault brought new sensations, and she shivered in his arms.

Adam shifted his weight, and before she knew it, Amelia felt herself sinking to the cooled grass.

"Oh, God, you feel so good," Adam rasped into her ear. With her head spinning from the bombardment of physical sensation, Amelia was amazed she heard him at all.

He rolled on top of her and Amelia reveled in the unexpected sensuousness of his weight. He rested most of his weight on his hands as he continued to rain kisses on her face and neck.

A moment later they rolled again and she lay atop him as his hands slid up and down the bare backs of her legs and up and over her rounded derriere. "This is much better without the liniment," he said.

Amelia didn't know when exactly it was that she realized they'd rolled onto the remains of the manure pile, but Adam seemed to come to the same realization at about the same time. "Son of a—"

"Eeewwww," Amelia moaned and scrambled to get off Adam, who was lying squarely in the middle of it. But in her haste, she slipped, falling fanny first into the muck.

Adam sat up, shaking his head. "Well, this pretty much kills the mood, doesn't it?"

Amelia managed to get herself up and stood there, trying to keep herself from gagging. She had cow manure

on her! For some reason, the only thing she could think
of was to get it off her. So, she unzipped her shorts and
let them drop to the grass.

Adam sat watching her, his eyebrows rising. "Or
maybe not."

Amelia then ripped her stained tee-shirt over her head
and flung it down to rest beside her shorts. Seeing . . .
no, feeling the smudges on her skin, she ran over to the
garden hose they'd been using to water the seeds after
they'd planted them and turned on the water. She aimed
the spray at herself and scrubbed at the spots she could
see.

She felt better just knowing the water was washing the
manure off her. Later, she'd scrub herself more thoroughly with soap, but for now, the hose did the job.

When she finished, she looked down at Adam, who
hadn't moved. "How can you just sit there in that?"

He grinned. "I don't know. Maybe because I just got
treated to a striptease and a wet-underwear show by a
beautiful woman."

Amelia looked down at herself in surprise. Her silky
bra and matching panties were soaked and clung to her
skin like, well, skin. There was absolutely nothing left to
the imagination and she felt herself blushing from her
chest to the roots of her hair.

"Oh my God."

Adam finally rose and took a few steps to clear the
aromatic pile of fertilizer. "Don't feel bad on my account.
I say we should do this more often."

Amelia stared at his grinning, sexy face and his ma-
nure-coated jeans and shirt and hit him full in the chest
with the highest setting on her garden hose. He recoiled

slightly, but didn't gasp or protest. Instead, laughing, he came after her.

"Don't you touch me," she shrieked. "Keep your cow-pattie-covered self away from me!"

He stopped and shrugged. "Okay. No problem."

He then pulled his shirt off and started on his jeans. Amelia would have protested, but she was staring at his bared chest, which was impressive, and his flat, hard stomach and his . . . jockey shorts. *Oh, my Lord,* she thought, *he's taking his clothes off.*

"Adam," she said rather breathlessly, "I don't think this is a good idea."

"I think it's a great idea," he countered.

Unable to take her eyes off the growing evidence of his desire, she didn't notice when her hand reflexively squeezed the handle of the garden hose and shot him with another blast of cold water.

He blinked in surprise. Amelia felt her mouth drop open. "Adam, I'm so sorry. I really didn't do that on purpose. It just . . . sort of happened."

Broad shoulders shrugged and Amelia watched the droplets of water run down his lightly furred chest and over his stomach, stopping at the waistband of his shorts, where the water disappeared. "Hey," he said, "things like that happen sometimes. Just like other things 'just happen' sometimes."

Before she could ask what he meant, even though she had a pretty good idea, the sound of a truck engine caused them both to turn their heads toward her drive. There, rattling toward them, headlights blazing, were Joe and Harry.

"Uh, oh," Amelia said. "There goes my reputation. Again."

Adam laughed without much humor and shook his head. "Yep. I don't think I can explain this away." He stared up at the darkening sky. "I don't know why I don't believe this," he said. Amelia had the feeling that he wasn't really talking to her. It sort of seemed that he was cursing the fates, or something.

"Maybe we should hide," she suggested. "Maybe they didn't see us.

He looked toward the truck, which had stopped about halfway down the drive, idling. "They see us," Adam assured her. "They're just deciding whether they should turn around and leave or barge on in.

The truck finally continued forward, coming to a stop next to Adam's truck at the side of the house, about thirty feet from where they stood. The lights of the truck went out and Adam sighed.

"Why does barging on in always win?" He looked over at Amelia, who still wanted to give running a try. He gestured toward the house with a nod of his head. "Why don't you go ahead and get inside while you can? The sight of you like this might be more than they can handle."

"Oh," Amelia squeaked and dropped the hose. She ran for the side door and managed to get into the house before Joe and Harry could get out of the truck.

She watched surreptitiously from the window as Adam nonchalantly walked over to the older men, who stood gaping at him while he tossed his soiled clothes and his boots into the back of his truck. They looked over at the house and nodded. Adam walked over to the side door and tapped on it.

Amelia hadn't turned the lights on and hoped neither of the older men could see her as she pulled the door open, keeping it in front of her. "Well?"

Adam shrugged. "I told them I slipped in the manure and that you slipped helping me up.

"And how did you explain our lack of clothes?"

"I told them the truth."

"The truth?" Amelia chirped.

"Well, sure. You freaked out because you got some cow dung on you and ran around like a chicken with your head cut off ripping your clothes off and hosing yourself down."

She stared at him. Now they thought she was an idiot. "And what about you?"

"I just said that I didn't want to mess up the inside of my truck."

Amelia looked past Adam to Joe and Harry, who stood together, talking in hushed tones, laughing when they weren't talking. "Great. Why did they come over here, anyway?"

"They wanted to check and see how the garden was progressing."

"Did you tell them it was done?"

"Nope. I told them that you had everything under control."

She rolled her eyes. "Like they're gonna believe that. I've been a walking disaster ever since I got here."

Adam chuckled and shook his head. "Not true. You're just . . . determined in a—um—unusual way."

"Whatever," she said curtly. "Look, they're leaving."

Adam turned to watch the two get back into the truck

and rumble away. Then he grinned at her. "Well, well, will wonders never cease? I don't suppose we could—"

"I don't think so," Amelia said with a laugh. "Regardless of what I just did, I really don't usually act like this, around men I hardly know."

He nodded. "Okay, I get it. I'll just mosey on back to my place and take a cold shower. Oh, wait, you already took care of that for me."

Amelia chuckled, glad that he wasn't annoyed or angry with her. "I didn't mean it. Really."

"That's okay," he assured her. "I'll let you make it up to me one day . . . after you've gotten to know me better."

He leaned forward and kissed her quickly but thoroughly and then left, loping toward his truck. Amelia shut the door and leaned against it. In the darkness of the kitchen, she could see six glowing eyes. She flipped the switch next to the door and the lights blazed overhead. Masha, Olga, and Irina stared up at her.

"I know," she told them. "I don't usually act like this. But it was kind of fun."

The sisters just stared at her, then Masha meowed and stalked toward the alcove behind the door. There sat empty cat food dishes and empty dog food dishes.

"All right." Amelia sighed. "I get it. Let me take a quick shower and I'll feed everyone. Where're Junior and Fife?"

A scratching at the door solved that mystery. She opened the door and the two dogs came in. Fife was shaking water from his tiny paws.

"Oh, Fife, did I make a puddle out there? Sorry. I'll be right back, gang."

With that she was gone upstairs and the animals sat staring morosely at the empty dishes.

Adam was whistling when he entered his house a few minutes later. Miss Amelia Appleberry was proving to be a much more interesting neighbor than he'd thought possible. This might turn out to be one very interesting summer.

He tossed his clothes into the laundry room and headed for the stairs when Jason walked in from the living room. His brother stared, then started laughing.

"What in the world happened to you? You left a few hours ago looking good and smelling pretty and now you stagger back here in your shorts"—he came a few steps to Adam and narrowed his eyes—"your wet shorts. How—wait a minute . . ." He sniffed the air and wrinkled his nose. "You sure don't smell like you did when you left here."

Adam wasn't about to try and explain what had happened to his brother. At least not right now. "Excuse me, Jason. I have to take a shower."

"I'll say you do," Jason retorted. "And don't think you're going to get away without telling me what happened to you tonight, brother," he called to Adam's retreating back.

"Smells like he's been rolling in manure," Jason muttered as he headed back to the living room.

Dawn came with an introduction via the rooster the next morning. Amelia frowned into her pillow as the rooster let loose with another bloodcurdling crow. She rolled over and groaned. "What? You haven't done this before."

From the foot of her bed, Olga stomped up to sit on her chest and stare at her indignantly. Amelia gazed at the cat through bleary eyes. "Don't blame me. I didn't put him up to it."

Olga didn't look satisfied and stalked away, swishing her tail in the air. Amelia sat up and stretched, yawning loudly. "And don't think I'm going to let you anywhere near that chicken coop," she called after the annoyed feline.

After taking a few minutes to wash the sleep out of her eyes and brush her shoulder-length, dark-brown tresses into a ponytail, Amelia got dressed in jeans and a light sweatshirt and headed out to the barn to feed her livestock. Junior and Fife stayed with her until they saw she was headed for the barn and then backed off.

"Once they get used to you guys, you'll be fine," she told the dogs. "I promise."

They weren't willing to take the risk yet and disappeared around the end of the house. Amelia turned her attention to the barn animals.

"Good morning, beasties," she called as she opened the barn door. The cow and the two horses poked their heads over their stall doors to look at her. "You know, I'm going to have to figure out your names," she told them. "I'm sure Aunt Gracie didn't just refer to you as cow, horse one, and horse two."

She opened the other barn door and then opened the stall doors to let them out. The cow plodded toward the back, her bell clanging loudly. "And don't go trying to escape again," Amelia called after her. She looked over at the horses, who both headed for the corral. "Now, you guys are so well-behaved."

The horses shook their heads and snorted at her.

Humming under her breath, she went from stall to stall, measuring feed and putting it in the troughs. Fresh water followed and then the mucking and the fresh hay.

The goat eyed her stoically as it stood waiting to be released. Amelia untied the rope and led the bleating creature out to the pen near the pigsty. She put the goat in the pen and shut the gate. "You know, you wouldn't have to be penned up if you'd just listen to reason and behave. A goat who wanders off all the time can't be trusted, you know."

He bleated in response and Amelia sighed. "I don't know. Nan and Ned said you weren't to be trusted. And after that stunt you pulled with Adam when he was only helping."

Another bleat and Amelia leaned over and scratched behind the goat's ears. "I'll think about it. But if you make me chase you down, you'll just have to go back to the big house."

She then let the goat out of the pen and allowed him to run loose. What could happen? If he wandered onto Adam's land, she'd just go and get him.

Adam. She smiled, then laughed out loud remembering how she'd unintentionally doused Adam with the hose. Then her cheeks pinkened as she remembered how caught up they'd been in each other just before that. If they hadn't rolled in the cow's contribution to recycling, who knew where it might have ended?

She heard a ruckus from the chicken coop and made her way around the end of the barn to check it out.

Built onto the side of the barn, the coop was a two-tiered chicken condo. Beyond that was a fairly large yard where the chickens could stroll, pecking at food and getting chicken exercise.

Amelia dipped some feed into a bucket and then flung it out onto the yard the way Nan and Ned had shown her. She then opened the little door to the coop and the chickens left their condo and fairly ran out to devour their breakfast, allowing Amelia to enter the coop and gather eggs. At least that was the way it had worked the last two days.

Not today. Today, the chickens left the coop, but the rooster stood at the door, taking a rather belligerent stance, it seemed to Amelia. "What? Are you having some sort of crisis? Are you feeling alienated? Is it the fact that you're the only male among all these females? And I have to say, I didn't particularly appreciate the crowing this morning. I mean, I'm normally an early riser myself, but another hour would have been greatly appreciated."

The rooster strutted, bobbing his head, eyeing her warily. She leaned against the side of the coop and looked out at the rest of the chickens. "You know, they don't seem to care that I come in and take their eggs. So, why should you? I swear, I'm not selling them or anything. They are strictly for personal use, which, granted, may seem rather barbaric to you. But, I *am* a vegetarian, so I should think that should give me a little leeway here."

The rooster bobbed his head again and then trotted out to the chicken yard to join the others in their mad pecking. "Thank you," Amelia called after him.

She gathered the eggs and took them into the barn,

where she placed them on a shelf. She then headed out to check on the pigs. She climbed up onto the railing and dumped their food into the trough and watched as they hurried over and began snuffling through it.

"Sadie, why are you the only animal with a name around here?"

The sow didn't answer her, but Amelia had a feeling that Ned and Nan probably knew, since they were the ones who had told her about Sadie. She decided that she'd drop by the Taxidermy and Cheese Emporium later and ask.

Just as she left the barn to head back toward the house, she saw a bicycle coming down her drive. It was Matt O'Brien, with Leo in the basket. He came to a stop in front of her, his freckled face beaming.

"Well, here he is. My mom says that if Leo learns not to chew, I can keep him."

"We'll do our best to make sure that he learns what he can chew and what he can't," Amelia promised.

Matt nodded. "Right. Well, I gotta get to school. I'll be back around three o'clock to get him, okay?"

Amelia reached into the basket and plucked the puppy from it. "That will be fine," she assured him.

Matt said good-bye to his puppy, then sped up the drive as Amelia and Leo watched. She then put the puppy on the ground and looked at him. "Well, Master Leo, are you ready to learn the ins and outs of doggy behavior?"

Leo shook his head, his ears flopping madly. Amelia laughed. "No? Well, that's too bad. Because you're going to anyway."

Junior trotted up then, and after some initial sniffing by both parties, a mutual acceptance was agreed upon and

Leo became Junior's shadow, nipping at him whenever he could and struggling to keep up.

"That's right, Junior," Amelia encouraged, "wear him out. Show him what being a dog is really all about."

She went back into the house and made some breakfast for herself and ate, then went out to survey her garden, carefully avoiding the manured area. Her clothes still lay on the grass nearby.

"Good Lord," she said. She really had just paraded around in front of Adam Larsen in her underwear. Make that her *wet* underwear. And then she'd seen to it, however accidentally, that he'd also had wet underwear. And now there wasn't much left to her imagination as far as his anatomy was concerned.

A wicked smile touched her lips as she thought about the possibilities. Then she shook her head. "Possibilities aren't probabilities," she told herself. "Besides, getting involved right now really isn't a good idea."

Junior heard her voice and trotted up to her. He sat at her feet and waved, studying her quizzically. Leo was right behind him, and he sat as well. She looked down at them. "I wasn't talking to you, guys. But since you're here, what do you think about getting involved with someone who I just met and who probably just wants me to sell my land to him and get lost?"

A sharp bark from Junior followed by a puppy yip from Leo was all she got in response. "I know," she said with a sigh. "But he's a really good kisser. And I have a feeling he'd be really good lover, too. Not that I'd be a great judge, considering my none-too-checkered past."

Junior didn't seem too concerned and yawned loudly before lying down. Leo nudged him, then gave up and lay down as well. Amelia had a similar reaction to thoughts about her romantic past. "Yeah, well, I'm still young; I've got time." She gazed beyond the garden and over the rolling hills of cultivated farmland to spy the silos and barns of the Larsen farm. "And opportunity," she murmured.

Fife appeared from around the house and growled. Amelia looked down at him. "Yeah, yeah. And too much hope and not a lot of common sense when it comes to sexy men like Adam Larsen.

Fife seemed less interested in Amelia's problems and more interested in the interloper, Leo. The two little dogs eyed each other, Fife indignant and Leo frankly curious. Finally Fife stalked off, refusing to have anything to do with the puppy.

"You'd be better off making friends," Amelia warned. "A bad attitude won't get you anywhere."

Fife looked back at her, his huge eyes watering as though he were about to cry. Amelia hurried over and picked him up. "Don't worry, Fife," she whispered, petting his shaking body. "I'll always love you more."

Two hours later Amelia approached Ned and Nan's Taxidermy and Cheese Emporium. She hoped she'd be able to handle the taxidermy part.

She pulled the door open and entered the rustic cabin. There was no one behind the polished wood counter and Amelia thought that was just as well. Because the place was odd. Spooky. Weird. Amelia didn't find too many things weird, but this . . .

The rough wood walls were adorned with the heads of

deer, elk, and moose, along with several different kinds of fish. In and on the various glass and wood cases in the store were other types of wildlife—like beavers, raccoons, squirrels, even a bear in the corner.

"Hey there, neighbor," boomed a voice and Amelia was startled out of her scrutiny of a hawk that dangled from the ceiling by some wires.

She whirled to see Ned, followed by Nan, emerging from the back of the store. "Hi," she said, "I was just, um, looking at . . . these," she finished, gesturing at the stuffed wildlife.

Ned beamed. "Yep, pretty lifelike, aren't they?"

Amelia could feel her eyebrows reaching for her hairline as she contemplated the glassy-eyed, stiff creatures around her. They all seemed remarkably dead to her, but she kept that opinion to herself. "They sure are something," she said instead. "How long have you been doing . . . this?"

Nan puttered over to the counter and picked up a dust cloth which she began using on the nearest display case. "Ned started this when he retired, didn't you, dear?"

"That's right. Fifteen years ago. Didn't know anything about it then. Messed up some carcasses, let me tell you. But I took some classes here and there and now folks bring me animals from all over the county."

Amelia nodded. "I can see that."

"And how's it going over at your place, honey?" Nan asked.

"Pretty well," she answered. "I've got the garden planted and most of my belongings are put away, or at least they're out of the way."

"That's good," Ned remarked. "How's that buncha weird animals you got?"

"Ned," Nan warned.

But Amelia wasn't offended. "They're fine. But I wanted to ask you both something. You said the sow's name was Sadie."

"That's right," Nan giggled. "Gracie named her after a lady she didn't like too much."

Ned laughed as well. "Yeah, that Gracie was a pistol."

"I know," Amelia agreed. "But do you happen to know any of the other animals' names?"

That seemed to catch them off guard. Ned looked over at Nan, who shook her head. "I don't think so," she said. "The only reason we knew about Sadie was because of her namesake. Gracie entered Sadie the pig in a county fair competition that Sadie the person was a judge at. Caused quite a stink—let me tell you."

"I imagine it did," she said neutrally, since she didn't know the Sadie involved. "But you don't remember her calling any of the other animals by name?"

They looked at each other and shrugged. "Not really," Nan said vaguely. "We didn't visit her when she was feeding the animals much. And she didn't—oh, wait, I think one of the horses was named Peaches or something. You know, I just can't remember."

Peaches? Amelia couldn't imagine either of those horses being called Peaches.

Ned offered, "The vet might have a record of them. I think Gracie used Doc Harris."

"That's a good idea," Amelia said. "Well, I have to be getting back. There are a lot of things I still have to do to get settled."

Nan held up a hand. "Wait a second." She hurried into the back room and came back quickly with a round of cheese and handed it to Amelia. "I want you to have this. Sort of a welcome-to-Hillview present."

Amelia figured it would take her months to finish a wheel of cheese that big, but she appreciated her neighbor's thoughtfulness. "I can't wait to try it," she enthused. "I've never known anyone who made their own cheese before."

"And if you ever need anything stuffed," Ned offered, "just let me know."

Amelia tried not to let her aversion to the very idea show in her face. "I'll keep it mind," she said and waved to them as she backed out of their macabre store.

"Okay," she said, as she walked toward her new home, "that was strange. Even for me."

A quick call to the veterinarian revealed that the horses were named Peaches and Herb, after the seventies music duo, and that the cow was named Wilhelmina. The goat and the other pig had no names of which the vet was aware.

Amelia hung up the phone and decided that the names would stay. Aunt Gracie had named them and must have had her reasons. The goat and the other pig, though, needed names. As well as the rooster. Not to mention the chickens.

Later that afternoon, as Amelia watered her newly planted garden, taking great pride in her accomplishment, she heard someone calling to her from the front of the house. She turned off the hose and headed around the end of the house to find a teenage girl standing in her drive, holding reins that led to a gentle-looking quarterhorse.

"Hello, there," Amelia greeted the girl, who looked about fifteen or sixteen.

"Hi," the girl replied. "I'm Kelly Owens. I baby-sit for Matt O'Brien."

Amelia nodded encouragingly, assuming that why the girl and her horse were here would soon be revealed. "I see. And how is Matt?"

"He's okay. He told some kids at school that you're helping his dog."

Amelia guessed she shouldn't have been surprised that the juvenile set of Hillview could spread gossip as fast as the adult set. "Yes, I am. Leo just needs to learn what he can and can't chew. I thought maybe my dogs could help him. Also, it will keep him out of Mrs. O'Brien's house for a couple of weeks."

Kelly nodded. "Right. Well, what I was wondering, was . . . do you think you could help Horace?"

"Horace?"

The girl indicated her horse. "Horace. He's got a kind of a problem."

Amelia eyed the docile horse. "He looks all right. And you do know that I'm not a vet, right?"

"Sure," she said. "Besides, Horace isn't sick. At least there's nothing wrong with him, physically."

"So, what is wrong with him?"

"He thinks he's a dog."

Amelia stared at the earnest expression on Kelly's face. The girl was serious. "Really? And why do you think that?"

"Well, it's like this," she explained quickly. "My folks

have a kennel and there've always been lots of dogs around. It wasn't until last year that they finally let me get a horse. But the thing was, after a few months, Horace didn't want me to ride him anymore, and I noticed him trying to get into the dog run and he tried to eat their food. Then one day he sort of barked—"

"Barked?"

Kelly shrugged. "It sounded like a bark to me. It wasn't a whinny or a horse snort—if you know what I mean."

Amelia lifted one shoulder and let it drop back. Why not? "I'm not sure if I can help Horace, Kelly, but if you like, you can leave him here for a few days. Maybe he can talk it over with Peaches and Herb."

Kelly frowned at her. "Who?"

"The two horses I recently inherited from my aunt."

"Really? Do you think it would help him?"

Amelia laughed. "I have no idea. But it wouldn't hurt to try."

Not exactly anything she'd planned, Amelia thought as they led Horace to the barn. But apparently, she was now boarding problem animals.

SIX

The day proved lovely, and just before noon, Amelia finished with her indoor chores and decided to go check on Leo and Horace. Just as she stepped outside, she heard the phone ring. She stepped back inside to get it.

"Hello?"

"Hi, it's Adam . . . Larsen," he added after a moment.

Surprised that he had called, Amelia nodded, then shook her head. Glad that he couldn't see her, she finally said, "Hi. How are you doing?"

Lame, she told herself. *What a lame thing to say.*

"I'm great, thanks, and yourself?"

She swore she could hear the smile in his voice. But was it just a smile, or was he laughing at her and her awkward attempt at telephone conversation? She'd never been good with the telephone, a freak in her generation of communications whizzes.

"I'm, uh, fine."

She closed her eyes. Telephone sales people were more welcome on the phone than she.

"What are you doing for lunch?"

That threw her momentarily, since she had been sure that Adam was about to hang up on her and call 911, thinking she'd fallen into a coma.

"Lunch?"

"Yeah, you know, the noon meal? Say, are you all right?"

Amelia squeezed her eyes shut and resisted banging her head on the wall. "I'm fine. I hadn't really thought about lunch."

"Good. How about a picnic?"

"A picnic?" Now Amelia wondered if she'd actually heard right.

"Mmm-hmm. There's a little pond on our property that's really pretty nice this time of year. I go down there when I get a chance. I thought you might like to join me."

"Sure," she said, glad he couldn't see her. A picnic, she thought as he told her that he would bring everything, a private pond, a blanket on the grass, probably some wine . . . "I'll never make it," she murmured to herself.

"What? Did you say something?"

Into the phone she replied, "Um, no, I, just, um, was wondering if I could bring anything?"

"Nope, I've got it all. I'll be over in a few minutes, okay?"

"Okay," she said. " 'Bye."

She stared at the telephone, wondering why she suddenly seemed to be dating Adam Larsen. Granted, they'd shared a few sparks here and there, but she had never intended for those sparks to ignite anything.

So, why had she agreed to go on a picnic with him? Because . . . because . . . "Just because," she muttered as she turned away from her contemplation of the telephone. She ran her fingers through her long, dark hair and abruptly jerked them out.

"Great."

She sprinted for the stairs, tearing her faded shorts and tee-shirt with the dog hair on them off as she ran. She yanked the door to her closet open and immediately dismissed everything in it. Then she took a step back and turned to face her reflection in the mirror over her dresser.

"Don't give this more weight than it deserves, missy," she warned herself. "He probably just wants to twist your arm some more to get you to sell your land to him."

Why that thought depressed her so much, she didn't want to consider. It was enough that she liked Adam and wanted to see him again. Actually, it wasn't enough, but it was all she had right now. And she liked the way he made her feel. So what if it were only temporary? So what if he abandoned her to her mini-farm and her menagerie when he finally realized that she wasn't going to sell?

She pulled a fresh pair of blue cotton shorts from her dresser along with a blue-and-white-striped tee-shirt and refused to think about all the reasons she shouldn't go on a picnic with Adam. A pair of white sandals completed her casual this-is-what-I-was-wearing-when-you-called ensemble.

A quick brush through her hair and a dab of lip gloss was all she had time for. She was grateful for good coloring and naturally long eyelashes as she heard the knock on the front door. Before she could get down the stairs, she heard Fife's high-pitched barking and Junior's happy yap. Another yip followed, and she remembered that Leo was still with them.

She pulled the front door open. "Come on in," she said quickly. "Don't mind the extra dog."

Adam looked down and saw Leo. "Right. The chewer. From yesterday."

Amelia nodded. "Right. He's not bored with Junior and Fife around to talk to, are you, fella?"

The puppy wagged his tail furiously and jumped up and down in puppy ecstasy at the attention she heaped on him. Then she looked up at Adam. "I guess I'm ready."

Adam nodded, then looked down at Leo. "Are you sure you want to leave the chewer inside?"

"He'll be fine," Amelia assured him. Adam didn't seem to understand the pack-animal mind, she thought. She had every confidence that Leo wouldn't do anything Junior and Fife wouldn't do. "Junior will be in charge and let him know what's what."

Adam didn't look convinced, but didn't pursue the point. "Okay," he said agreeably.

He stepped out onto her front porch and held the screen door open for her. Amelia stepped over the threshold and walked down the steps. Adam hovered on the porch.

"Aren't you going to lock the door?"

Amelia looked at him in surprise. "Why? Do I need to?"

He stared at her. "Well, most people do."

"Uh-huh. There a lot of crime around Hillview? Break-ins and such?"

Adam shook his head. "No, actually, it's a very safe community. But you should still lock your door. No sense inviting trouble."

Amelia shook her head. "It'll be fine. Besides, I haven't had a chance to install doggie doors yet. What if something happened and the dogs couldn't get out? I'd feel much worse than if someone stole something from me."

Adam apparently didn't have an argument for that and shook his head as he came down the steps toward her. Amelia turned, expecting to see his pickup truck parked next to her van, but was surprised to see a saddled horse instead.

"Using an alternate form of transportation today, Adam?"

"Actually, yes," he explained. "The pond isn't easily accessible except by foot or horse. And better his feet should walk it than mine. I didn't think to ask earlier: Do you ride?"

Amelia nodded. "Yes. But I haven't in a while."

"Do you want to ride with me or would you rather saddle one of Miss Appleberry's nags?"

Amelia became indignant on behalf of the "nags." "I beg your pardon. Those horses happen to be purebred Arabians."

She gestured toward the pasture she'd turned the horses into earlier. Adam looked, but the horses weren't in sight. "Whatever you say. I'll take a quarterhorse any day."

Amelia looked toward where the horses had been a while ago, and frowned. "Where are they?"

"Maybe they saw me and Duke here and decided to hide."

"Duke?"

The horse bobbed his head up and down, as if acknowledging his name. Amelia, unable to resist any animal, came up to him, her hand extended, and gently rubbed his head between his ears. "You're a handsome guy, aren't you?" she told the horse. He let her run her hands over the hide of his neck and through his mane.

"So," Adam said after a moment, "I guess we should both ride Duke, since we can't even see your horses."

Amelia nodded absently. "They're there. They just want some time with Horace, I imagine."

"Horace?"

She turned to look at him. "Yes. A girl named Kelly brought him by this morning. Apparently, Horace is under the assumption, despite his half-ton size, that he is actually a dog."

Adam didn't challenge her on this, and, to her surprise, he didn't even laugh. "A dog?"

She nodded, glad that he seemed to understand Horace's predicament. "Right. At first, I was skeptical, but then we took Horace up to the barn and he didn't want to go in when he saw the other horses. But he was ready to run off with Junior and Fife when he saw them. Poor Fife almost got stepped on."

"So, what are you doing with this horse-dog? Or is he a dog-horse?"

She narrowed her eyes at the seemingly sarcastic question, but Adam seemed guileless.

"I walked him around and then I put a saddle on him, but he didn't seem to like it. Then I decided to keep him away from the dogs and let him spend the morning with the horses.

"Okay," Adam said. "So, we can both ride Duke. He doesn't mind."

Amelia was sure he wouldn't. She watched Adam mount the horse with an ease born of practice and then extend his hand toward her. She only hesitated a moment before reaching out her own hand.

His hand grasped her wrist and forearm and pulled and Amelia felt herself leave the ground in a surreal flying motion. Then she plopped down behind Adam, one arm clutching at his waist, the other at his shoulder for balance.

"You all right?"

"Sure," Amelia said, shifting her weight in an attempt to find a more comfortable spot. But the back ridge of the saddle was in front of her and saddlebags which no doubt contained a picnic lunch, were behind her. She hoped this pond wasn't far.

Duke started moving then and Amelia tried to remain cool, her hands lightly placed on the ridge of the saddle in front of her. That lasted until Adam urged the horse into a canter. Fearing a spectacular fall, Amelia wrapped her arms around Adam's firm waist, her chest plastered against his back.

"How are you doing?"

"Just fine," she told him. "Just where is this pond of yours?"

He raised his right arm and pointed westward. Amelia couldn't see anything in particular. "It's over that way," he said. All Amelia could see in that direction were acres and acres of crops and some trees farther out.

"So, how long does it take to get there?"

He shrugged and Amelia felt his muscles moved against her breasts. She moved backward, trying to put some space between them while still holding on for balance, but discovered it wasn't possible. So, she leaned on

his back and tried not to think about what he'd looked
like yesterday with water dripping down his bare chest.

She heard his voice and tried to concentrate on that.
"It's hard to say. Depends on how fast you go, but on
horseback, maybe ten or fifteen minutes."

It didn't sound like a long time, but she still wanted to
distract herself.

"What did you bring for lunch?"

He laughed. "Let it be a surprise."

"You remembered that I'm a vegetarian, didn't you?"

"Yes, I remembered," he said. Then, "Did you remember to water your garden this morning?"

"Yes, I did," she said. "The book said some of the
plants might come up in about a week or so."

"That's about right," he told her. "What are you going
to do in the meantime?"

She couldn't tell if he were laughing at her or not, so
she chose to believe he wasn't. "I have a lot to do in the
house still, and there are the animals. I have to name
some of them."

"Name them?"

"Yes, some of them apparently don't have names."

Adam turned his head slightly and Amelia could see
his profile. He had a straight, rather elegant-looking nose,
she thought absently. With his square jaw and slightly
shaggy hair, he was what might be termed *rugged*.

"I didn't think about that," he admitted. "I'd go over
there and check on them, but I didn't know their names.
And I never asked. Except for Sadie, of course."

"Of course," Amelia echoed. "I talked to Ned and Nan
this morning. Apparently there was quite a rivalry between the woman Sadie and Aunt Gracie."

"All I really know is that they didn't like each other," Adam informed her. "And that during one of their many set-tos, Miss Appleberry named her sow after Miss Wilkins."

"Actually," Amelia said, "I know some of their names. The horses and cow were listed with the vet, so she told me their names. But the goat and the other pig and the chickens all need names."

"The chickens?"

"Of course," she said firmly. "How am I supposed to have any kind of rapport with an animal without knowing its name?"

He didn't say anything for a moment, then grunted, "I guess you couldn't."

They continued in silence, a silence that made Amelia more and more aware of Adam and the hard contours of his back and waist. *More conversation,* she told herself.

"So," she said, as effortlessly as she could, "do you have any ideas about what I should name them?"

He turned his head to look at her in surprise. "Me?"

"Well, why not you? You've been around them more than I have. They must have revealed certain personality traits to you that might help with coming up with a name."

He shook his head. "All I know is that you have to make sure you don't turn your back on the goat or he'll butt you and that the rooster has an attitude problem and no sense of time. The chickens are just chickens, and the pig is a pig."

"Okay." She sighed. "You're not being helpful at all."

"Sorry," he said, sounding anything but. She tried not to hold it against him. Not everyone understood the importance of names. Mostly they just didn't acknowledge it.

"So, why *Duke?*"

"What?"

"Why *Duke?*" She repeated. "Why did you name your horse *Duke*? Why not *Lightning* or *Buttercup?*"

"Because he looked like a—okay, okay," he said. "I get it."

"Thank you," she chirped. "So, I need to find names that fit their personalities."

After a moment, Adam said, "Well, this may sound stupid, but that rooster reminds me of Don Rickles."

Amelia burst into laughter. "That is so perfect. He's loud and obnoxious, but it's really just an act. That's it. Rickles."

The next few minutes were spent naming the various chickens after celebrities. It wasn't until the horse stopped walking that Amelia realized that they'd arrived at the pond. She peered around Adam's broad back and almost gasped.

"Oh, Adam. It's lovely."

"I think so," he said proudly. "My father and brother and I did some landscaping and clearing one year when I was a kid. It was an anniversary present for my mother. She used to love to come here for picnics."

"I can understand why."

The pond sat in a shallow valley, surrounded on three sides by a small copse of trees, which created a sheltered, private area. The grass surrounding the pond was a perfect shade of green and looked plush and soft.

Adam reached around and grasped Amelia's arm and helped her off the horse before dismounting himself.

Amelia barely got her balance before she kicked off her sandals and let her toes sink into the cool grass.

She fairly skipped down to the water's edge and waded in up to her ankles. She turned back to Adam. "Do you ever swim here?"

He stood next to Duke, the saddlebags in his hands, an oddly intense expression on his face. Amelia froze, unsure of herself. What had she missed? Then he smiled and it was almost as if she'd imagined it all.

"Um, sure, I swim here sometimes. It's not very deep, so you can't really dive; but sometimes, when I just want to get away and cool off, I come here and jump in."

He freed a rolled-up blanket from behind Duke's saddle and unfurled it, then placed it under the shade of a nearby oak tree. The saddlebags he set on one corner of the blanket to anchor it, then walked down toward the water where Amelia still stood, watching him.

"If you want to swim, you're more than welcome. Anytime. It's better if you don't go alone, though. Even though the water's not deep, it's enough to drown in."

Amelia looked at the water in surprise. "I suppose so. But to tell you the truth, I doubt that I could find this place on my own."

He chuckled. "It's not really a mystery spot. Just look for the trees beyond the corn fields and you've found it."

"I'll, uh, keep it in mind," she said, suddenly awkward as she looked up into his eyes. In those blue depths gleamed a barely contained desire that almost made Amelia gasp in its intensity. She suddenly felt flushed and uncomfortable in her own skin. Unused to this level of sexual attraction, Amelia felt out of her league. So she chose to do what she usually did when she didn't know what to do in a situation. She pretended it wasn't happening.

"So," she said, a bit too breathily to her own ears, "what's for lunch?"

Adam paused, then lifted one eyebrow, telling her in no uncertain terms that he knew exactly what she was doing. It remained to be seen if he would let her get away with it. Amelia hoped he would. She really didn't need any confrontations right now.

"Lots of things," he said slowly, a small smile playing at the corners of his mouth. "Potato salad and fresh-cut vegetables and fruit and bread and cheese and wine—"

"Good Lord," Amelia exclaimed as he began pulling small containers of those items from the saddlebags. "How much food do you think we could eat at one sitting?"

He shrugged. "I didn't know what you might like or not like, so I figured I'd just bring a little of everything."

"I guess so," she laughed as she picked up one of the containers. "Did you do this or did you have someone else do it?"

He didn't try to hide his guilt. "I confess. I went to the deli at the supermarket and got it."

Amelia plopped down on the blanket and crossed her legs tailor fashion. "I'm impressed with the spread," she said, accepting a napkin rolled around silverware from him. "I've never been on a catered picnic before.

"Only the best to welcome Hillview's newest resident."

Amelia looked up in surprise. "I guess I am a resident now, aren't I? I hadn't really thought of it that way."

He settled on the blanket and handed her a paper plate, then began opening the containers of food. "I wasn't really sure about that. I mean, you said that you didn't know how long you might stay. Have you changed your address and all with the DMV?"

Amelia blinked at him. "No, I haven't. I hadn't even thought about it," she admitted. "I guess I should do that, huh?"

"That depends on what your plans are," he equivocated. "Are you going to stay here in Hillview or are you just here for the summer?"

That was a question Amelia had asked herself countless times. And the answer still hadn't become clear. "I don't know," she said honestly. "I haven't really had much time to think about the future. I mean, I know that that's why I'm here, but with unpacking and taking care of the animals and planting the garden . . ."

Adam laughed. "That's understandable. You've only been here a week. And you have been busy."

She nodded eagerly. "I know. And that's been great. I haven't had time to brood over my problems."

"I can't see you brooding," he teased. "You don't seem like that type."

Amelia chewed on a piece of french bread and eyed him. "Really? And what type do you think I am?"

"Well," he drawled, "from what I've seen so far, you seem more the get-an-idea-do-it-now-think-about-the-consequences-later type."

She laughed lightly. "That sounds like you think I'm impulsive and flighty."

"No," he denied, "maybe just a little narrowly focused. Sometimes."

She considered that. "I can't see the forest for the trees?"

"Maybe."

"Okay, I'll give you that. Sometimes the reality of a situation has to bite me on the behind before I get it. But what about you?"

He gazed at her warily. "What about me?"

"Don't I get to venture an opinion as to what type you are?"

Grinning, he gestured expansively. "Venture away."

Amelia narrowed her eyes and gazed at him pensively. "I think," she said slowly, "that you are the type of man who knows to the dollar how much money he has, how much mileage is on his vehicle, exactly how many rows of corn he has, and where all the receipts are for all the purchases he's made in the last few years."

He stared at her as she spoke, his discomfort evident. "Are you saying you think I'm uptight?"

Amelia shook her head vehemently, "No, no, I didn't mean it that way. You just seem like the type who's probably . . . organized and . . . thorough."

He slowly leaned forward until he was nose to nose with her. Amelia saw that gleam return to his eyes. "I can be very . . . thorough," he said softly, and Amelia felt her skin break out in gooseflesh as she shivered deliciously.

Without a snappy comeback, she could only nod. "Really?"

"Definitely," he said.

"Well," she said, then stopped to clear her suddenly obstructed throat. "Hmm, I suppose . . ." She couldn't look away from his eyes and she lost her train of thought. "What was I saying?"

"I have no idea," he said, as he closed the short distance between their lips.

As she was quickly learning, Adam's kisses tended to cause a suspension in her personal space-time continuum. However, since she had never experienced kisses that provoked such powerful longing in her, she wasn't willing to stop, even when she knew she should.

Just as she felt herself about to give up on reality altogether, Adam ended the kiss, leaning back to gaze at her through heavy-lidded eyes. Amelia found swallowing difficult under a smoky gaze that was every bit as disturbing to her as his kisses were.

"You're a dangerous woman," he murmured. "Did you know that?"

She shook her head, realizing that he was teasing; but there was also an undercurrent that she couldn't quite identify, an edge to his voice that made her think he believed what he said.

"Not me," she denied. "You're the dangerous one. I've only been here a week and I'm behaving . . ."

"How are you behaving?" Adam prompted.

Amelia cleared her throat and took a deep breath. "Like someone else."

His smile was wicked. "Someone else? Do you have her phone number?"

Amelia laughed and shook her head. "What I meant was that I don't usually . . . that is, I . . . well, it's just different for some reason."

"Some reason?"

She eyed him warily. His questions seemed like casual conversation, but Amelia sensed something else beneath the surface. "That would be *you*," she said bluntly.

He appeared to consider her statement as he unwrapped a sandwich and took a bite. Then he leaned back on his elbow and looked up at her.

"Are you saying you're attracted to me?"

Amelia closed her eyes and shook her head. Then she opened her eyes and said, "Duh."

Adam laughed. "Okay, maybe that was a dumb question. So, why do you think you're behaving like someone else?"

"I don't know," she said. If she believed in love at first sight . . . suddenly, before her brain could short-circuit her mouth, she was speaking, "Do you believe in love at first sight?"

A sense of dread descended over her as she realized what she'd just said. She had nowhere to hide and she couldn't very well take it back. Still, she wasn't quite prepared for Adam's all-too-quick response.

"No. I think it takes a time to know if you love someone. But I do believe in lust at first sight. Maybe that's it. Maybe it's just chemical."

"Chemical?" She didn't know why, but his adamantly negative opinion about love at first sight annoyed her. Why did he have to dismiss the very idea so quickly? Because he was too logical and too rational, she thought. Probably really wrong for her in every way. He didn't seem to notice her introspection and continued with his theory.

"Yeah. You know, a chemical reaction. The type that burns itself out quickly. Of course, it has to be ignited first."

Amelia already felt rather hot. But she was willing to banter for the sake of lightening the atmosphere. "Sorry, but I don't have any matches."

He smiled again and she felt like hitting him. No one should be able to affect anyone else that way just by smiling. Then he said, "Lady, you are a whole book of matches."

"Yes, well," she said primly, inexplicably pleased by his compliment, "let's just say that flammable items should be placed out of the reach of children so they don't burn down the house."

"Or themselves?"

Amelia nodded. "Or themselves."

He took another bite of his sandwich and chewed contemplatively. "How long until we can play with them?"

Amelia longed to put an end to the veiled comments and tell him that she would like nothing better than to take him into her bed today. Forget the bed, this blanket would do just fine. But she clung to the single scrap of common sense she possessed, knowing that she didn't want to have regrets about Adam. So, she toyed with a container of potato salad and sighed.

"I don't know. You're probably right. It probably takes a while to know a person well enough to make those kinds of decisions. For all I know, you just want to seduce me so that I'll sell you my land."

She hadn't really intended to be so blunt, but once the words were out, once again, she couldn't take them back. However, this time she wasn't sure she wanted to.

Adam didn't move. It was a deceptive stillness, as it didn't affect his turbulent blue eyes. She thought he was angry, but couldn't be sure. Finally, he pressed his lips together, then said, "I would never do that."

Amelia nodded. "I believe you. At least I think I do. I want to. But, as I said, I just met you. And while you seem to be a nice guy, you're also a guy who wants my land."

"Yes, I do," he admitted quietly. "And I'm not going to stop trying to get you to sell it to me. But I'd never lie to get it. I would never use you to get it."

Amelia trusted her instincts above anything, and right now her instincts were telling her that Adam could be trusted. But could she be sure that it was really her instincts and not just her libido talking to her?

"You know what the sensible thing to do is, don't you?"

He looked at her warily. "I thought I was the sensible one here."

She let one eyebrow lift slightly before saying, "Very funny. I'm not going to deny that sensibility isn't a high priority to me. You, however, are the soul of practicality, aren't you?"

He looked uncomfortable. "I guess I'm practical. But not to a fault."

She ignored his qualification. "So, what do you think the sensible, practical thing to do is?"

Adam watched her for another moment before heaving a big sigh. "That would be to back off and not have sex until we know each other better and you learn that you can trust me not to seduce your land out from under you."

"Very good," Amelia praised.

"You wouldn't want to define exactly what *sex* is, would you?"

She rolled her eyes at him. "Don't even go there. You know exactly how far too far is."

He laughed. "Yeah, I guess I do. So, how long do you think—"

"I don't know," Amelia cried, laughing. "I'll let you know.

"Are you sure you won't forget? Do you want me to remind you?"

Her laughter faded as she saw the purpose in his eyes again. "Believe me," she whispered. "I won't forget."

Adam nodded once and pushed up from his elbow to sit facing her. He reached out and cupped her chin and kissed her sweetly. "Good. Now," he continued, "what else can we talk about? Have you thought of any names for that goat?"

"Maybe I'll name him after you," she quipped.

"Why," he asked, leaning back and picking up the remains of his sandwich, "because he's so charming?"

"Because he's stubborn. But in a cute way," she retorted.

"Cute?" he scoffed. "Men aren't cute. Women are cute. Kids are cute. Kittens are cute. Men aren't cute."

"Well, too bad," Amelia told him. "There are a lot of things I don't know about you, but one of things I do know is that you're cute."

"What else do you think you know?"

She shrugged, willing to go along with him. "Well, as I said, I think you're stubborn. But in a good way. And loyal. And a gentleman—I told you that already. And you like animals. That's a really big one with me."

"Really? I never would've guessed," he teased. "Since you think I'm a gentleman, doesn't that go back to the trust thing . . ."

"Yes," she allowed, "but trusting you not to take advantage of me while I'm unconscious and trusting that you won't take advantage of me while I'm awake are different things."

He nodded slowly. "I'm sure that you meant whatever it was that you just said."

Amelia thought that she'd been perfectly clear. "And don't you forget it."

The following evening Amelia glared at the growing mound of clothes in her hamper and, resigned, retrieved her laundry basket and transferred the clothes for their trip to the laundry room behind the kitchen.

Sorting through the clothes, she heard a crinkling sound. Delving into the pockets of several items, she finally found the culprit. A bright blue piece of paper folded twice. She unfolded it and smiled. It was the flyer she'd picked up at the diner. *The King and I* at Hillview High.

She picked up the phone and dialed the Larsens' number. No one was home, so she left a message for Adam to call her. She then stuck the flyer on the front of the refrigerator and went back to her laundry.

Sometime between the rinse and spin cycles of the second load, the phone rang. It was all Amelia could do not to grab it on the first ring. "Hello?"

"Hi, Amelia, it's Adam."

"Hi. I know it's short notice and all, but I was thinking about going to see *The King and I* tonight and wondered if you might like to come along."

A telling pause lasting several seconds made her smile. He was desperately trying to come up with an excuse, she thought.

He finally said, *"The King and I?"*

Amelia laughed. "I know it's only a local high school production, but I think it might be fun. But you don't sound as if it's exactly your idea of entertainment, so I'll just go by myself."

"No, no," he broke in. "I guess I was just surprised. I didn't even know about it and I live here."

Amelia wasn't sure if he was making that up or not. "There are flyers up all over town."

"Oh. Right. Maybe I've seen them—but didn't really pay attention. You really want to go?"

"Yes, I do. I think it'd be a great way for me to meet more people and see some of ones I've already met again."

"Okay. What time is it?"

Amelia started to feel guilty. "Really, Adam, you don't have to go. I just thought—"

"I don't have any other plans, specifically," he told her. "So, when should I pick you up?"

She told him and hung up, glad she had someone to go with, but guilty that he was obviously only going because she wanted to.

"That's okay," she told herself as she went upstairs to shower and change. "I'll do the same for him someday."

The play started at 7:30, so they stopped by the diner for a light dinner first. Their waitress appeared a bit harried when Amelia asked about Dori.

"She's over at the school right now spraying goop onto the hair of a dozen children."

Adam's only reaction to that announcement was a

raised eyebrow. The waitress then lifted her eyes from the order pad and looked at him. "Hi. How're you doing, Adam? What can I get you? Don't ask for the meatloaf."

Amelia ordered a salad and Adam, a turkey sandwich. After the waitress departed, he looked at Amelia. "I didn't realize you knew Dori Sanders."

"Well, I don't, not really. I stopped in here for lunch the day I got the book on gardening. She was very nice and offered some tips. Her daughter is in the play."

He nodded and they made small talk about the diner and how it had been a hangout for decades in Hillview and how it changed but somehow stayed the same. Thirty minutes later it was time to leave for the high school.

Adam drove confidently, pointing out various sites as they passed them until they turned into the rapidly filling parking lot of Hillview High.

"High school plays must be popular around here," Amelia marveled, seeing the number of vehicles in the lot. "I can remember plays when I was in high school that weren't nearly this well attended."

Adam's smile was a bit lopsided and Amelia felt an almost overwhelming urge to kiss him. "You didn't grow up in a small town, did you?"

She shook her head, trying to focus on his words instead of his lips. "Uh, no, I didn't. Suburbia. It's not a pretty world, but most of us survive it."

"Well, most of us who grew up in small towns have much the same attitude. But one thing we can say—we get a good turnout for almost any live performance of anything we do from kindergarten on.

Amelia laughed as Adam grasped her hand and steered

her through the parking lot toward the crowded entry to the auditorium.

No fewer than a dozen people hailed Adam and several more shook his hand in greeting or slapped him on the back. And every one of them glanced curiously at Amelia. And she saw each of their eyes widen as Adam introduced her as Grace Appleberry's heir.

They got their tickets and made their way to their seats with more people stopping Adam and more curious looks at Amelia. Finally, they sat down and Amelia turned to him.

"So, do you actually know every single person in Hillview, Wisconsin?"

He laughed. "Probably. Though I think they only greeted me as a polite way to find out about the beautiful woman with me."

It should have sounded like a line, but to Amelia it didn't, and she found herself beaming at him. The lights began to dim then and they turned their attention to the stage.

As high school productions went, it wasn't too bad, Amelia reasoned as the play went on. The Siamese accents weren't quite within the grasp of Hillview's teenage set and the scenery sometimes wobbled or moved the wrong way, but overall, it was entertaining. Lucky for the audience, the kids were all at least adequately musical. And "The March of the Siamese Children" got a huge round of applause as the littlest cast members ran out to strut their stuff.

When the standing ovation—led by relatives and friends, but still hearty—was over, Amelia sighed and turned to Adam. "Thank you for coming with me. I know that you didn't really want to be here."

Adam held her hand in his, as he had for most of the performance, and squeezed it. "Oh, I don't know. It wasn't that bad. I think *I* should thank *you* for inviting me."

The crowd began to thin and they made their way up the aisle to the lobby only to find a throng of people mobbing the cast and crew of the show, who'd come out to meet and greet their public. Children from five to eighteen, dressed in elaborate costumes, were congratulated by what seemed to be a steady onslaught of well-wishers.

Adam tried to escape the crowd, but was pushed back by a line of the King's children. Amelia saw Dori then, standing in a group of people with many of the children. She turned to Adam and said, "I won't make you stay, but I'd like to say hello to Dori."

"No problem," he assured her. "The parking lot's more jammed than the lobby."

She squeezed his arm and turned toward Dori. Just before she got to her, Dori turned and saw Amelia. "Hey," she cried, "you actually made it. You are one brave newcomer to our humble town."

"It was great," Amelia said and meant it. "Didn't you think it was?"

"Sure I did, but I'm partial."

Dori reached out and snagged a passing small person and gestured to the painted child with the black hair. "This is the reason I'm here. Tiffany, this is Amelia."

"Hi," Tiffany chirped before being dragged away by two friends.

Amelia laughed. "Nice hair."

"Thank you very much." Dori grinned. "Did you come alone? Some of us are going out in a little while."

Amelia was touched that she was included, but shook her head. "Actually, I got Adam Larsen to come with me."

Dori craned her neck and spotted Adam talking to several men who appeared to be waiting for wives, children, dates, or the parking situation to ease. "My, my. Adam Larsen. You really must have something on him. I don't think he's been back in this building since graduation. What did you do to get him to come?"

Amelia shrugged. "I asked him."

"Good approach. Hey, I'd better go track down my little Siamese child before she rubs her head against something and stains it."

Amelia waved and promised to stop in the diner again soon, then turned back toward Adam. He saw her and broke away from the masculine group holding up the auditorium wall and met her in the middle of the lobby. "Ready?"

She looked up at him and thought that he was the kindest, sweetest, sexiest man she'd ever met. "Yes," she murmured with a smile she couldn't contain. "I'm ready."

SEVEN

It was almost a week later that Amelia felt the thrill of seeing her first seedling.

She'd established a nice morning routine that involved the feeding and inspection of the animals and their quarters followed by breakfast and then a look at the garden. She'd peer anxiously at the dirt, wondering when, or if, her seeds would become plants.

This particular morning, however, she peered down at her garden and actually saw a few tiny green shoots poking out of the dirt.

"It's happening," she cried to no one except Junior, Fife, and Leo, who had followed her out here as usual. She turned to them, eager to share the moment.

"Look, guys! It's the seedlings. They're here!"

Junior barked happily and dashed from one end of the garden to the other while Leo wagged his tail furiously and tried to nip the older dog as he raced by. Fife trembled and stared, his huge eyes watering.

"I know," Amelia continued, "I'm excited, too! One thing to remember though—no digging in the garden. If you have to dig, go somewhere else. Okay?"

They all appeared to acquiesce, and Amelia turned back to her garden and sighed with a deep sense of satisfaction. It had worked. She'd planted the seeds and they'd taken root. It had actually worked. And she owed it all—well, a large part of it—to Adam.

They'd gone out to dinner one night and to a movie another night. Amelia was having such a good time that she pushed the doubts away.

After their last date he'd left her at her front door with a searing kiss and a promise to call her if she hadn't called him by the end of the week.

It was technically both, since it was Saturday, but Amelia had tried not to think about Adam and, of course, thought about him constantly. She tried to concentrate all her attention on putting the house in order, caring for the animals, and meditating on her purpose for being here—namely figuring out her own future. But that just seemed so daunting that she found her thoughts drifting, mostly to Adam Larsen and his kissable lips and sexy eyes.

She made her way back to the house, and after taking Zilla off the stove and placing her on the window sill, she picked up the phone and then put it down. He wouldn't be there anyway. Saturday wasn't a day off on a farm.

"Well, Zilla, what should I do?"

The iguana blinked at her.

"Right. Get my mind off him."

Two hours later, dressed in her favorite blue jean shorts overalls and a crop top, she was climbing up to the hayloft in the barn, chasing Rickles, who'd escaped through the open door when she'd gone into the coop to gather eggs and had taken refuge in the barn.

"Come on, Rickles, get back to the chicken yard where you belong.

The little rooster hopped up onto the sill of a window and sat there, bobbing his head at her.

"You'd better be careful. Chickens can't really fly, you know, despite the wings."

He clucked loudly and, Amelia thought, rather indignantly. She didn't want to frighten him with any sudden moves; but when she took a slow step toward him, he flapped his wings in a panic and fell out the window.

Fear clutched at her as she rushed to the window and looked down. There, directly below her, was the chicken yard; and standing on top of the chicken coop about ten feet below her was Rickles. He was still flapping and making bawking noises, but he looked fine.

"Think about this the next time you decide to check out how green the grass is elsewhere." Rickles then flew the short distance down to the yard and strutted around as if nothing had happened.

Amelia looked up and realized that she could see quite far from up here. She could see Ned and Nan's across the road, even though she had to peer through some trees. And she could see the pasture where Wilhelmina, the cow, and Peaches and Herb lounged with Horace, who was either coming to grips with being a horse or thought the others were just big dogs like him.

Farther out, she could see acre upon acre of cultivated farmland. Larsen farmland, she reminded herself. As far as the eye could see.

She looked over her shoulder and saw the other window opposite her. She walked around the hayloft to it and looked out, seeing her aunt Gracie's house and the garden, which really was a speck compared with the vast acreage farmed by Adam Larsen.

She looked toward the east and saw the silos and barns of the Larsen farm. From here she could see quite a bit. She could even see the pond if she leaned far enough out the window and looked to the south.

"I wonder where Adam is," she said to herself. And what would she do if she knew where he was?

"Nothing," she thought as she headed down the ladder. As much as she wanted to tell him about her garden coming up—or was it coming in?—she would just have to wait. It wasn't the sort of news likely to be considered important by a real farmer.

She stopped at the bottom of the ladder and looked around. The barn was mostly empty. With the cow and horses out in the pasture, that only left Cy, the goat. Amelia had decided to call him the Ultimate Recycling Animal, since he'd eat anything, and then shortened the name to Cy.

"Hey, Cy, are you being a good goat today?"

He stared at her as he chewed on a piece of hay. She'd stopped tethering him to his stall after she'd explained to him that wandering off would just cause trouble for all concerned. She suspected that it was more force of habit that made him stay in the stall than anything else.

"Come out of there and get some exercise," she told him and pulled the unlatched door to his stall open wider. "You know, you could've butted your way out of there anytime. You're making real progress."

Cy clambered to his feet and bleated at her as he walked toward her. Amelia let him follow her to the pigpen. She felt a real sense of satisfaction when Cy didn't try to butt her.

She climbed on the railing of the pigpen and looked in at her expectant charges. But Sadie wasn't in her usual spot. Abner—Amelia had no reason behind that name; he just looked like an Abner to her—was snuffling in the trough, and Amelia had to look around before she spotted Sadie. She lay in a dryer corner of the pen, and there were two tiny piglets next to her—and another emerging as Amelia watched.

"Oh, my gosh," she exclaimed, "the piglets!"

Cy stuck his head through the lower slats of the pen to see what all the commotion was about. But it must not have seemed very interesting to him, because he wandered out into the pasture as Amelia stood there, yammering incoherently.

"What should I do? Nan and Ned said I didn't have to do anything. But what if they're wrong? What if something happens and I don't know what to do to help?"

The first thought that came to her was to find Adam. He might think her crazy for it, but she really didn't want to risk Sadie or the piglets because of her ignorance.

"Hold on, Sadie," she called to the sow, who blinked proudly at her. "I'll be right back."

With that she hopped off the fence and ran to the house. She called the Larsen farm, but the machine picked up. She hung up and wondered how she'd ever find Adam, then she remembered the hayloft. Maybe, she thought as she raced to the closet, she could spot him from the barn.

She dug through a box in the closet until she found what she was looking for, a pair of binoculars. Then she hurried out to the barn and climbed up to the hayloft. It didn't take long to find out where Adam was working. At least she thought it was Adam. It could have been Adam.

It was a group of men. One of them was probably Adam. One of them turned to speak to another and she saw that shock of burnished golden-brown hair and knew it was he.

They weren't too far from the border of her property, she noticed. It was easy to see that, because there was a fence that snaked along the border, cultivated Larsen fields on one side and uncultivated pastureland on the other. And the fence was only about five acres from the barn. And they were working about ten or fifteen acres farther away maybe. That really wasn't that far, she thought. She could get there in a few minutes. Less than that if she rode one of the horses.

That thought sent her scurrying down the ladder and running into the pasture, yelling to the sow as she passed the pigpen, "Don't worry, Sadie. Everything's under control!"

She ran into the pasture and spotted Peaches and Herb grazing quietly under a tree. Horace stood farther off, watching them. Amelia made her way toward the horses, walking quickly, but trying not to startle them.

"Hey, Peaches, how'd you like to give me a bareback ride?"

The horse twitched her ears at Amelia, but stood still for her as she patted her neck and shoulder and then grasped her bridle and led her over to a tree stump, which she used to boost herself onto Peaches' back.

"Okay," Amelia said softly as she settled atop the horse. "Now, listen, Peaches. I haven't ridden bareback

in about ten years, so I'd appreciate it if you'd help me
out in the balance and direction departments."

Peaches shifted her large ears again and waited. Amelia
grasped two handfuls of mane and leaned forward
slightly. She rested her bent legs along the horse's side
and then gently squeezed with her thighs. Peaches responded by starting to walk forward. Amelia experienced
a moment of triumph.

It wasn't as difficult as she'd feared. Peaches responded
easily to Amelia's direction and started to trot on cue.
Amelia didn't think she was really ready to try cantering
yet, so they trotted all the way to the border of the Appleberry land.

"Oh, no," Amelia groaned when she saw the barbed-
wire fencing.

She slowed Peaches with a tug on her mane and sat up
straighter, looking along the line of fencing. "Leave it to
Adam Larsen," she muttered. "Not a strand of wire out
of place or a fence post down."

She slid off Peaches and walked up to one of the fence
posts, giving it a good shake. It didn't budge. She sighed
and turned to Peaches, about to concede that maybe it
wasn't meant to be, when she saw something.

The next post over, on the top row of barbed-wire—
what was hanging on it?

She hurried over and plucked the pair of wire cutters
from their forgotten perch. She tried to consider that she
probably shouldn't do it, but what if something actually
happened to Sadie because she was incompetent and
didn't even know enough to know when things had gone
wrong?

So—with a bit of struggle—snip, snip, snip, and the

fence was open. She pushed the wire out of the way and went back to get Peaches. Amelia carefully used a fence post to remount the horse, then they continued onto Larsen property.

It took very little time to find the men, who were repairing some piece of machinery. They were only about a half a mile away and were making quite a bit of noise. Amelia discovered that there was a small road that snaked through the acreage, so she didn't have to take Peaches in amongst the beans. Or whatever it was that was growing.

The men—Adam, Joe, Harry and two others Amelia hadn't met—looked up in surprise when they saw Amelia and Peaches trotting toward them. Adam pulled a handkerchief from his back pocket and wiped the sheen of sweat off his face as he came toward her.

Amelia stayed atop Peaches and looked down at Adam. "I'm sorry to interrupt you, but Sadie is having her piglets and I'm afraid that something might go wrong."

Adam squinted up at her in the morning sun. "Is she in some kind of distress?"

"Well, how should I know?" Amelia reasoned. "She didn't look happy, but I don't really know what a pig looks like when it's giving birth."

"Maybe you should call the vet. I'm not much of an expert myself. I raise crops, not pigs."

"I used to work on a hog farm," Joe piped up. "Want me to go take a look for you?"

Amelia nodded gratefully. "Would you? I mean, it may be nothing; but if it is something and I didn't do anything, I'd feel terrible."

Joe nodded and glanced at Adam, who shrugged. "Go take a look."

Amelia looked at Joe gratefully. "Thank you so much. Do you want to ride Peaches back?"

Joe practically jumped. "No! I mean, I'll hoof it, if you don't mind. Won't take too long."

Amelia was about to protest because of the time that could be saved by riding, but Harry stepped forward then and said, "Joe's afraid of horses."

"Am not," Joe protested hotly while skirting Amelia and Peaches. "Just don't have no use for the derned things."

"I'll come over as soon as we finish with this," Adam said, jerking his thumb at the large piece of machinery. Amelia nodded and turned Peaches around to follow the rapidly disappearing Joe.

She caught him moments later and again offered him a ride and was again turned down.

"I'll get there just fine without having to climb up on one of them beasts," he declared. "You go on ahead. I'll be there in no time."

Amelia could see that arguing with him wouldn't do any good.

She urged Peaches into a trot and was soon back on her own property. She rode the horse right up next to the pigpen and slid off, letting Peaches wander back to Herb and Horace.

She got up on the rail and looked down at Sadie, who was right where she'd left her, only surrounded by three more piglets.

"Sadie!" Amelia exclaimed. "You have five babies— wait, six," she corrected, seeing one piglet that two others had obscured.

Ten minutes and two more piglets later, Joe showed up

and peered over the railing at Sadie. Amelia pointed and said, "How many piglets should she have?"

Joe scratched his head. "Well, seeing as she only has, uh—room—to feed eight of 'em, any more are pretty much out of luck."

Amelia knew that nature was often cruel and that she shouldn't let it get to her emotionally, but she counted the piglets again and felt true relief that there were only eight.

"Uh-oh," Joe sighed.

Amelia groaned. "Nine." Another piglet emerged and joined the rest in the tussle for food.

Joe climbed over the railing and slowly approached Sadie. "Keep an eye on ol' Papa there for me," he told Amelia, who looked over at Abner, who stood snuffling at the trough.

"Why? He's quiet and—"

"Because he's a hog and they can get testy if you get in their pens when their female hogs is having babies."

Amelia thought that made a certain amount of sense. "All right," she agreed. Then she turned to Abner. "Okay now, Abner. Joe's just going to take a look at Sadie and your babies to make sure that everything's all right. Then he'll leave. So don't worry, okay?"

Abner looked at her, then looked over at Joe, who froze in his tracks. Then the hog turned back to the trough and continued his snuffling. Joe looked at Amelia and shook his head before continuing toward Sadie.

He looked and even did a bit of prodding and pushing. Sadie didn't seem to care. Except for a few snorts, she didn't acknowledge Joe's presence. Finally, he headed back toward Amelia.

"Well, that's it," he said, as he swung his booted foot

over the rail. "I don't know how many of 'em will make it. That's a nature thing. Something you just can't predict."

Amelia didn't like the sound of that. "What can I do? How do you know?"

Joe scratched his scruffy beard. "Well, sometimes one or two will get pushed out, see?"

"You mean rejected by Sadie? Why would she do that?"

"You gotta look at it from her side. If pushing one out makes sure the others live, then that's what she has to do."

Justification of it didn't make it seem better to Amelia. "There has to be something we can do if it happens."

Joe looked uncomfortable. "Uh, you know, it's pigs."

"I know," Amelia said, trying to be philosophical. "I know that they're raised for food and that it's survival of the fittest and all that, but I just feel that I should do something. I don't know if I could just stand by and let nature, you know, take its course."

Joe shifted from one foot to the other and readjusted his cap. "Well, I have heard about folks who've taken runts and fed 'em by hand and all, but it don't always work."

Amelia looked at the piglets, so tiny and helpless, unable to see or care for themselves. And one of them was going to be rejected by its mother. Life just wasn't fair.

Adam got back to the house and found it empty. Jason was probably already gone for the day, even though it was only a little after one in the afternoon.

He checked his machine for messages and then went

up to take a shower and change into jeans and a tee-shirt. He considered calling Amelia to see how her sow was doing, then decided to just go over there. Joe had never returned and Adam was afraid that might mean bad news.

There were several vehicles parked in front of the Appleberry farmhouse. Besides Amelia's van, he saw Doc Harris's truck and the O'Brien truck and Harry's truck and a bicycle.

Adam stopped on the front porch to knock, but didn't. The commotion inside the house made it a pointless endeavor. He looked through the screen door and saw several people moving about, all of them talking at once. Most of the activity seemed to be centered in the kitchen, at the end of the hall in front of him.

He pulled the door open and went inside. Matt O'Brien came barreling down the stairs carrying a towel and ran into him. Adam reflexively steadied the boy.

"Sorry, Mr. Larsen."

"What's going on, Matt?"

The little boy's face was alive with excitement. "We're trying to save the runt."

With that he dashed off in the direction of the kitchen. Adam nodded to himself and thought it odd that he had a pretty good grasp of what that meant. He continued toward the kitchen and then stopped in the doorway, taking in the barely controlled chaos.

Amelia and Doc Harris stood over a box on the table. Joe and Harry stood to one side, offering unsolicited advice, while Maggie O'Brien cooked something on the stove.

"Okay," Doc Harris said, "you have to keep him warm and fed constantly. And this still might not work."

"I know," Amelia conceded, "but I couldn't bear to just let him die."

Joe whacked Harry on the arm. "You shoulda seen her, Harry. When that runt got shut out, she got all worked up, and the next thing I know, she was in the sty, picking the little devil up and telling me to call Doc Harris."

Harry rubbed his arm. "I know, already. You done told me six times."

Maggie O'Brien turned to Amelia, "The evaporated milk is warmed. What are you going to put it in?"

"Do you have a baby bottle?" Doc Harris asked.

"No," Amelia said, dejected.

"How about rubber gloves?"

She brightened at that and ran over to a drawer. She returned with a yellow glove. "Will this do?"

Doc nodded. "For now it will. We'll just put some milk into the glove, puncture the end, and the rest is up to PeeWee here."

"Hey, that's a great name," Matt exclaimed from his perch on a nearby chair.

"Matthew, get down before you fall and break your neck," his mother warned.

Matt sat down, but he wasn't happy about it. Then he spied Adam by the door. "Oh, I forgot. Mr. Larsen is here."

Adam watched everyone suddenly turn and look at him. "Sorry I couldn't get here sooner," he offered.

Amelia nodded at the box. "Well, it was only about an hour or so ago that this poor little guy got kicked out of his pig family. I wanted to try and save him if I could."

Joe reached Adam's side. "You shoulda seen her, Mr. Adam. She just hopped right into that sty—"

"Yeah, Joe, I heard," Adam told him. "You been here the whole time?"

The older man looked indignant. "It ain't like I been trying to get outta work. But you shoulda seen Miz Amelia. She was downright, uh, whatchacallit—"

"Distraught," Harry supplied.

"Yeah. Downright distraught. I thought I should stay and help out if I could."

Adam nodded, trying not to smile at the older man's arguments of sincerity. "I'm sure Amelia appreciated your input."

Harry pulled on Joe's sleeve. "How long since you checked on the rest of the litter?"

Joe looked momentarily stunned; then he ran for the door, Harry hot on his heels.

Doc Harris gathered up her bag and keys. "I have to get going now. If you have any trouble, page me."

Amelia nodded. "Okay. Thanks for coming out here, Annie. He's not taking the milk, though."

"Try giving him a little through an eyedropper or small baster. It may take awhile. But be prepared for the worst."

Adam watched as Amelia nodded, a sheen of tears in her dark eyes. *She's gone all sentimental over a pig,* he thought. *What would she do with a child of her own? She'd fight long and hard for any child! She'd be a great mother.* But did she know it? He doubted it.

Doc Harris left and Matt, spotting the opportunity, pulled a chair up and, once he'd climbed up on it, peered into the box. "He sure is little."

"Most babies are," Amelia told him, ruffling his hair.

Maggie laughed. "My baby here weighed almost ten pounds when he was born."

Amelia eyes widened. "Ouch."

"Come on, Matt," Maggie urged. "Go get Leo. We have to get home now. You have a ball game this afternoon."

Matt yelled a hasty good-bye and raced out the door, calling for Leo. Maggie paused at the door. "You know, I really want to thank you for whatever you're doing with Leo. That dog hasn't chewed anything except rawhide bones since he started coming over here. I hope you don't mind, but I gave your number to a woman from our church. She has a cat who won't leave her bird alone. I thought maybe you could do something."

"I'm not sure, but I could try, I guess," Amelia said.

"See you later, Amelia. Adam." After some brief good-byes, they were alone.

Adam walked over to look at the piglet. It was indeed little. Just a few inches long and pale pink, its eyes not yet open, and rejected by its mother and siblings. "Life's tough, ain't it, PeeWee?"

Amelia rummaged through another drawer until she came up with a small baster. She filled it partway with milk and dropped a bit of liquid on the piglet's mouth.

"I hope he doesn't die," she murmured.

Adam wished he could tell her he wouldn't, but the odds were that the little piglet would be dead before morning. Not wanting to dishearten Amelia, he spoke encouragingly. "I'm sure he won't," he said. "Not with you on his side."

She gave him a watery smile, and Adam suddenly wanted to hug her to him, to kiss her, to make love to her. But since any of the above would most likely get him smacked, he just reached out and gently squeezed her shoulder.

"Thanks," she whispered before turning back to Pee-Wee.

It was just after midnight when the little piglet Matt and Doc Harris had named PeeWee finally started to eat. Amelia had been using the baster to drop evaporated milk into his mouth every fifteen minutes; but while he accepted that bit of nourishment, he hadn't taken to actually feeding himself via the glove.

Adam and Amelia hadn't given up yet and, as a relatively safe way to pass the time, had started playing Scrabble.

"What does *qwerty* mean?" Adam demanded.

Amelia shifted her tired bottom on the unforgiving kitchen chair. "You know, the keyboard nickname."

Adam just looked at her. Amelia had come to enjoy those looks. He challenged her a lot; and if they'd really been playing by the rules, she'd have been toast. "Keyboard nickname?"

"Yeah," she insisted, going for the full lie. "The first row of letters on English keyboards—q-w-e-r-t-y. So office workers adopted the word. You know, as in 'My qwerty needs cleaning' or 'I spilled coffee on my qwerty and now it doesn't work.' "

He gave her a hard look. "You are so full of it, you know that? I bought your definition of futurepast, and even photolistic, but this one—"

The sucking sound went unnoticed for a moment as

Amelia tried to argue her case. "But, really, Adam, that's what they call . . ."

She stopped talking abruptly and gazed into the box at PeeWee, who sucked away at the milk-filled glove she'd left near his mouth.

"Oh, Adam, look. He's eating!"

Adam rose and leaned over Amelia's shoulder. His chest barely brushed her back, but she felt as if something was squeezing her from her chest to her knees. It was difficult to breathe and her heart beat alarmingly fast. Which really wasn't much of a surprise to her. The sight of him, the scent of him, the thought of his lips kissing hers had kept her preoccupied all night.

After the others had left, they'd watched a little television in between watching the piglet do nothing, then had started playing Scrabble. Amelia figured it was a safe enough game until Adam started forming words like *position* and *pliant* and *climax*. It was difficult enough trying to think around him without his making it that much more difficult. And she needed a distraction before a perfectly innocent game of Scrabble turned into Strip Scrabble.

And now . . . now PeeWee showed signs of fighting. The relief she felt was overwhelming. "Maybe he'll really be okay."

Adam hummed, then said, "Maybe."

Amelia turned and looked up at him. "I know that his chances aren't good, Adam, but isn't it good that he's eating?"

He nodded. "Sure. Sure it is. I just don't want you to get your hopes up," he said before sighing and touching her chin. "But it's too late for that, isn't it?"

She shrugged one shoulder. "Yes, it is. But really, it has to be a good sign. He just needs us to believe in him and not give up on him."

Adam looked down at the tiny creature. "Well, then he's probably going to be fine. Because I have the feeling you're as stubborn as they come."

She didn't think that was an insult. "I'm not stubborn," she insisted. "I'm determined."

"And you're good with semantics." He chuckled. "Whatever you're doing, it seems to work. How do you do it?"

Amelia looked down at the tiny animal and shook her head. "I really didn't do anything special. I know that I have a rapport with animals, but I don't know why or how it works."

"You seem surprised by your own success, but I can't imagine why. What with all your own critters plus Leo and that horse, and now Maggie's friend's cat."

"I have no idea," she answered honestly. "I'm not really sure I am doing anything special."

"Well, you're doing something, and they must think it's special," Adam insisted. "Because you are very successful with the animal set. Like this one," he added, pointing at the now furiously sucking piglet.

Amelia felt the compliment down to her toes. "I am, aren't I? But I don't know why."

"Maybe it's better not to analyze it," Adam suggested. "Some things in life can't be explained; and the more you try to figure them out, the less you understand them."

Amelia looked up slowly; and when her gaze met his, he knew what she was thinking and it had nothing to do with animals. In less time than it took her heart to skip a beat, Amelia was in Adam's arms, reveling in his kisses, burning for his touch.

She didn't know what it was about Adam that was different from other men she'd known or dated. But there was an intangible sense of urgency that filled the air whenever she was with him. She didn't know why it happened; but when he touched her, kissed her, she lost all reason. And didn't miss it.

His hands slid down her back as he urged her closer, and Amelia went willingly. It felt so right in Adam's arms. Nothing else mattered.

Adam's fingers touched the skin of her waist where her crop top left a few inches of bare skin at the sides of her overall shorts. Amelia felt shivers race over her skin and she gasped, feeling Adam's smile against her lips.

His hands crept under the overalls and played over the skin of her waist and back. "Your skin is so incredibly soft," he murmured against her cheek.

Her own hands kneaded the hard muscles of his shoulders and upper arms, giving lie to a restlessness she'd felt since she'd first laid eyes on Adam Larsen. She felt his hand pressing against the small of her back, urging her hips into his, and she felt his arousal, hard against her belly. She felt her own body's answering heat gathering within her, yearning to be released.

A tiny voice tried to warn her that they were going too fast, too soon, but Amelia tuned it out.

She didn't even notice when her overalls were unclipped and the bib and back fell to her waist. His lips never left hers as his hands slid around to span her ribcage and then move up to cup her breasts, gently holding them as his thumbs caressed her nipples.

He seemed to know exactly where and how to touch her to give her the most pleasure. Amelia's hands wandered restlessly over his chest and shoulders, up to the nape of his neck, where her fingers tangled in his hair. She loved touching him, loved the feel of his smooth, lightly hair-dusted skin.

Adam pulled back then and took a long deep breath, his hands still resting on her waist. "Okay, do I stay or do I go?"

It took Amelia a moment to understand what he was talking about. "Oh," she said, her face pinkening, "I—um, that is, do you want to go?" She suddenly felt insecure and hoped he wasn't going to say yes and go, leaving her alone and frustrated.

Adam stared at her, chuckling, then hugged her to him. "No, sweetheart, I'd really like to stay."

She pressed her lips to his throat and touched her tongue to his rapidly beating pulse point. "Then stay."

They made their way upstairs, taking the box holding the now sleeping PeeWee with them. Amelia placed him in a corner of her bedroom with a lamp warming the box. She stood and turned to find Adam watching her. "What? You think I'm silly for doing all this for a pig?"

He shook his head. "No, not at all. I think you are very caring and maternal, and it's too bad you only have animals to devote your energy to."

Amelia felt a familiar yearning swell within her at his words, but she pushed it aside. Hoping too much for something usually caused disappointment. Instead, she tried to remain optimistic, without letting her longing overwhelm her. "Maybe," she said now, "someday."

Nodding, he reached out his hand to her. Amelia knew

that if she had any sense, she'd say it was too soon and that there were too many unresolved issues between them. But the only sense she had around Adam was a sense of need. She needed and wanted him and she felt safer with him than she'd ever felt. That meant something, although she wasn't quite sure what. So she took his hand and let him pull her to him, next to her bed.

He kissed her gently, sweetly, and Amelia felt her bones turning liquid. He kissed her again, and again, becoming more demanding and giving more when she made demands of her own.

Adam's hands slid over her bottom and pulled her against him. She felt his desire for her, and her desire for him, coiled deep within her.

Their clothes fell to the floor around them as their hands sought buttons and snaps and zippers, pausing to explore exposed flesh as they went. Finally, they stood naked, gazing at each other in the dim light, breathing deeply.

Adam touched her cheek with his finger. "You're sure?"

Amelia nodded and kissed his palm. "Very sure."

They sank onto the bed together and Amelia felt free of doubt about herself for the first time in ages. As Adam's hands skimmed over her body, learning her secret pleasure spots and kissing her breath from her, she knew that she hadn't done anything this right in a long time.

They explored each other, stroking and kissing and licking until each moaned with pleasure. Adam whispered her name as he told her how beautiful and desirable she was and Amelia felt helpless to do much besides urge him closer.

When he finally rose over her, she opened herself to him, and as he slowly entered her, Amelia felt strangely complete. And free. Free of doubt and inhibitions and filled with a sense of hope and trust.

For Amelia, the pleasure they shared went far beyond heart-stopping, breath-snatching physical passion. Although there was that . . . a lot of it. Even more important to her were the whispered words of encouragement and the spontaneous muffled laughter that erupted. They urged each other further and further until Amelia felt buffeted by the storm of their lovemaking. She felt herself about to give in, then clenched her muscles around Adam and let herself go.

The spasming of her body around him was enough to take Adam over the edge and he surged into her one last time, a low groan of pleasure escaping his throat. Amelia, her breath coming in little gasps as she held him tightly to her, felt herself returning to earth and tried to forestall the inevitable. She didn't want to think about what she'd just done and she didn't want to wonder about how Adam felt. She just wanted to let the moment go on, suspended within them for as long as she could.

Adam pulled away from her long enough to rearrange their bodies so that he was lying behind her, spoon fashion. He lightly stroked her still-quivering body and planted a kiss here and there on her back, her shoulder, her neck.

"That was perfect," Adam whispered into her hair.

Amelia nodded, almost afraid to talk. "I know."

She wanted to say more, to tell him more, to ask him

more, but she was afraid of what he might say and what he might not say. So she fell silent. And so did Adam. And then they didn't have to think about what to say. They fell asleep holding each other.

EIGHT

Time took on odd properties for Amelia. It sped up or slowed down, mostly due to Adam Larsen and his presence or the insane amount of time she spent thinking about him.

They fell into a routine that she wouldn't have expected to like. Mostly because Amelia didn't like routines. She liked spontaneity and surprises. But there was a certain comfort in knowing that she was going to see Adam almost every evening for dinner and sometimes for lunch. Still, it didn't seem like enough. The fact that he also spent almost every night that week in her bed was beside the point.

"You know, Kojak," she told the bird as she gave him fresh water and food, "I don't know what's wrong with me. Maybe it's that I still haven't come close to finding my purpose in life. I haven't even devoted any real time to thinking about it, either."

The balding bird squawked at her and flapped his wings, causing more feathers to leave his body and drift to the floor of his cage. Amelia sighed. "I don't know. I've been busy with the garden and with Leo, who's doing great, and Horace, who doesn't bark anymore, and the house and all. But am I really just keeping busy so I won't have to face coming up with a career?"

Kojak offered no real insights. "Who loves ya, baby?" he chimed in his weird monotone. Amelia stared at the bird. "Is that it?" she asked, more to herself than to Kojak. "Am I falling in love? No, it takes time to fall in love, doesn't it? At least more than a few of weeks. Doesn't it?" Amelia had never been one to err on the side of caution, but this time was different. If she didn't know herself well enough to know what career was right for her, how could she trust herself to know when she was really falling in love? "Isn't that right, Kojak?"

Kojak clammed up. Amelia left the living room and headed through the house to the kitchen and out the side door, Junior, Fife, and Leo right on her heels. She made her way around the house to her garden, where she surveyed with satisfaction the progression of her plants. It was a constant battle to keep the weeds at bay, but she was pleased with her efforts.

"But I don't think I'm a farmer, guys," she said to the canine trio lying on the grass. She'd gotten only a glimpse of the vast amount of work that went into running a farm the size of Adam's and didn't think she was up to the business management, crop management, irrigation management, labor management, and heaven knew what else Adam dealt with so well every day.

So if farming wasn't her calling, what was? Nothing came to mind. That didn't surprise her, since she'd never been able to come up with a career. If she hadn't managed to think of anything in twenty-five years, what made her think it would just suddenly come to her now?

The sound of a car and crunching tires on the gravel

offered her the opportunity to think about something—anything—else and she welcomed it. She headed around the house to see who it was, the three dogs trailing her, Fife having to run twice as fast just to keep up.

There, in the driveway, was Mrs. Kappelman, the owner of the bird-hating cat. She was a sweet old woman, and Amelia had been happy to help her. And Klaus had made some real progress.

"How's my little Klaus?"

"He's fine, Mrs. Kappelman."

"Can I take him home today?" she asked anxiously.

Amelia nodded, "I think so. Klaus hasn't bothered Kojak at all for two days."

"That's wonderful," the elderly lady exclaimed. "Really, when Maggie O'Brien said you were a whiz with animals, I wasn't sure; but you're really great. You have a gift."

Amelia led Mrs. Kappelman to the house. "I don't know about that," she demurred. "I just love animals and try to understand why they have whatever problem they're having and then try to come up with a workable solution."

The older woman clapped her hands together in delight. "Like a psychologist—only for animals!"

Amelia had never really thought of it that way, but it made sense. "I suppose so."

They entered the kitchen and headed for the living room. There, on the sofa sat Klaus, with Olga, washing their paws. Kojak sat on top of his cage, ignored by the cats.

"There we are," Amelia announced.

"Klaus! Sweetie, Mama's come to take you home."

Klaus looked up with disinterested feline eyes, but he

jumped lightly off the sofa and walked over to rub against Mrs. Kappelman's ankle. She stooped and picked him up. "Are you all better, now? Not going to chase the bird anymore?"

"I'd keep an eye on him for a few days, Mrs. K.," Amelia advised. "Just in case temptation becomes too much for him."

Mrs. Kappelman beamed at her. "You're a wonder, Amelia Appleberry; that's what you are. Everyone in town is talking about how you can get animals to behave. You really should advertise."

Amelia laughed. "If everyone in town knows, I won't have to advertise, will I?"

They both laughed. Then Mrs. Kappelman pulled a piece of paper from the handbag that dangled from her elbow. "Here."

It was a check for twenty dollars. Amelia protested, "No, Mrs. K., this isn't necessary."

"Pish tosh," Mrs. Kappelman insisted. "You provide a service, you should be compensated for it. If you don't value your abilities, no one else will, either. My father taught me that when I was a little girl. Well, I have to be going. Pinochle is at my house tonight. Will I see you at the shindig next weekend?"

Amelia held the door for the old lady. "The what?"

"The Farmers Association Banquet and Dance. Or whatever they call it. I'm surprised Adam Larsen hasn't asked you to it with him. Him being president of the local Farmers Association and all. He's such a nice boy. You got the cream of the crop with that one, dearie. Anyway, they have it every year. It's a pretty big deal. I met Mr. Kappelman at one fifty-two years ago. He was the new science teacher, you know. It was love at first sight, for both of us."

Amelia, her thoughts filled with why Adam hadn't asked her to this dance, nodded absently. "Really?"

"Oh, my dear, yes. Sometimes you just know the minute you meet someone." Her blue eyes twinkled merrily. "Of course, what really clinched it was the way he kissed. Oh, boy!"

"I know," Amelia sighed. Or at least she thought she knew. But should she trust herself? "Did you date him awhile before you were really sure?"

They walked out into the yard, Mrs. Kappelman shaking her head. "Oh, no. We were married a few months after that. What's the point of waiting? I mean, that's all right for some people, I suppose, who aren't sure. We all have to follow our own hearts. But if you know it's right, go for it. That's what I've always done. Can't say I've had too much to complain about."

Amelia waved good-bye a few minutes later as Mrs. Kappelman and Klaus drove away. Too much to think about, she decided.

Should she say something to Adam about the dance? Maybe he just hadn't gotten around to asking her. Absently she looked down at the check she still held in her hand.

"I can't cash this," she muttered as she made her way back into the house. She put the check on the kitchen table and considered Mrs. Kappelman's words. Did she really have a gift? Even if she did, what did that mean, if anything?

"Right now, it doesn't mean anything," she said to herself. "Because right now I have to go muck out the barn and check on the piglets."

Speaking of piglets, she hurried to the box in the corner next to the stove and peered in at PeeWee. He blinked up at her and oinked his tinny little oink. She opened the refrigerator and removed a small baby bottle with some milk in it and popped it in a pail of water on the stove.

"I'm on it," she told the tiniest piglet. "I can't believe how much you've grown," she crooned to PeeWee, who squealed up at her. Amelia had been so relieved when PeeWee had accepted the milk and hadn't starved to death. Now he was still tiny, but he'd put on a few ounces and Doc Harris thought he was going to be just fine.

After the milk warmed, she reached down and lifted the box, piglet and all, and placed it on the table. She offered him the bottle and he sucked it greedily. "Little pig," she joked, glad that no one was there to hear her poor attempt at humor. PeeWee didn't care.

"You know, I'm going to have to get you a pig-sitter for next Saturday night. Provided Adam actually asks me. Maybe I'm assuming too much about him. Maybe he doesn't feel what I feel."

What exactly did she feel? she wondered. That was one thing she didn't want to think about. Because she might find out something she didn't want to know. Or she might find out something that Adam wouldn't want to know.

Late the next afternoon, Wilhelmina went missing again. Over the past couple of weeks, the cow had disappeared from the pasture only to reappear later and Amelia had no idea where she'd gone or how she'd gotten there or how she'd gotten back. This time, Amelia determined she would look for the absent bovine.

"OK," she said to Junior as they stood at the entrance to the pasture. "Do you see her?" Junior looked around, woofed, and waved at her. "No? Me, neither. Well, you're part shepherd. So, do your stuff. Herd."

Junior just stared at her, his tongue lolling out the side of his mouth. Amelia sighed. "OK. How about just looking? Where's Wilhelmina?"

That elicited a sharp bark and Junior took off into the pasture. Another bark came from behind her just as she started to run after Junior. It was Fife, standing near the edge of the barn.

"No, Fife," Amelia said. "You stay there and, uh, guard the barn."

The little dog growled, but stayed put. Amelia turned and hurried after Junior, wondering if he really could find the cow or if he were just playing.

It turned out that the shepherd part of Junior must have been dominant, because he led her straight to the fence where she'd cut through the barbed wire a week before. "Oops," she told no one in particular, "I think I forgot to tell Adam about that."

Junior waited at the cut fence, wagging his tail. At his feet were hoof prints. Evidence of a recent cow escape? "Good boy!" Amelia praised. "Now, go find Wilhelmina."

It occurred to her as she made her way onto Larsen land that the hoof prints could've been made by Peaches and were a week old, but it had rained since then, so she had confidence that they were cow prints and not horse prints.

"How would I tell the difference?"

Not an expert on the variances between horse and cow hooves, Amelia figured that even if Wilhelmina hadn't wandered over here, it was still worth the look.

Junior took her on a zigzaggy trip through corn fields that bore evidence of some large animal. Stalks had been trampled and there were more hoof prints. After a while, Amelia began to feel lost. The corn stalks were as tall as she and the only guide she had was a dog who'd never been here, either.

Still, she trusted Junior and they pressed on. It wasn't too much longer that they came upon one of the roads that crisscrossed the Larsen farm. Junior turned around a few times in what looked like a joyous dance of discovery to Amelia. "Okay," she said to the happy dog, "now what?"

Junior trotted away, headed down the road—or was it up the road? Amelia wondered how long it would take her to find Wilhelmina. She had to get back and feed PeeWee in an hour or so. How long would it take to walk all the way to Adam's house? It had to be a mile away from where she was.

Fortunately, ten minutes later, she heard the approach of a motor and turned to see Joe and Harry coming toward her in their rattletrap of a truck. Harry slowed when they saw her and Joe waved to her from the passenger side.

"Hey, whaddya doing out here? You could get heatstroke," Harry called.

Amelia walked up to the truck, putting her hands on the door at the open window. "It's not that hot. And I was just looking for Wilhelmina."

"Who?"

"My cow. Junior and I"—she waved toward her dog, who sat patiently next to her—"are hot on her trail. Have you seen her?"

Joe and Harry looked at each other and shrugged, shaking their heads. "Nope," Joe told her. "We ain't seen no cows. But, then, we've been over to the west of here."

Harry suddenly had an idea. "Why don't we give you a ride up to the house? Maybe your cow's up there."

Amelia nodded. "Maybe." She cast a surreptitious glance at the interior of the truck cab. It was beyond dirty. Apparently, Joe and Harry weren't too particular about how much dirt they rode around in. Then she looked through the back window into the truck bed. It looked beaten up and there were a few farm implements in it, but it looked cleaner. "Junior and I will just hop in the back."

Before they could object and offer her a seat up front, Amelia hurried to the back and pulled the tailgate down. She signaled to Junior, who leaped up into the bed of the truck without having to be asked twice. Amelia perched on the gate itself, hanging on to its chain for support. "OK, guys," she called out. "Not too fast."

They were at the house just a few bumpy minutes later. The truck pulled up next to one of the barns, and before she could hop off the tailgate, she saw Adam step out of the barn and look at her with a surprised expression.

"Amelia. What are you doing riding around with these two?"

The two in question had hustled out of the truck and come around to meet them. "We found her walking along the east road looking for a cow."

Adam just raised his eyebrows and looked at Amelia, who nodded. "Yep. That's what I was doing. Junior and I tracked Wilhelmina to your property. She's been disappearing lately and I wanted to find out where she's been going. Have you seen her?"

He shook his head and pressed his lips together. He appeared to be about to laugh at her. She didn't know why; she hadn't said anything funny. Not yet. "No," he said instead, "I haven't. And since the property is fenced, I don't see how she could've wandered over here."

Amelia laughed then, but it was a nervous sort of giggle. "Ha, um, there's an interesting story there. See, remember when I came over last time, when the piglets were born? I kind of cut through the wires then to get through."

He gaped at her. "You cut through my fence?"

"Well, the wire cutters were right there, hanging on the fence. I thought it was like Divine Providence. You know, meant to be. So, anyway, I guess I forgot, in all the excitement, uh, about the fence."

He sighed, then looked over at Joe and Harry. "Can you guys get over and fix that fence? Amelia and I will look around for her missing cow."

"Sure, boss," Joe assured him and tugged on Harry's arm. "We'll get right on it, won't we, Harry?"

Harry jerked his arm away. "Let go a me. I'm coming already."

Joe let go, but jerked his thumb at the truck. "Well, then, let's go."

Junior jumped out of the back of the truck as Joe and Harry slammed their doors. They drove away and Junior barked and ran off behind the house.

"Junior's hot on Wilhelmina's trail," Amelia explained.

"He's a funny looking bloodhound."

"Well, I told him to herd her, so that's what he's trying to do. But he has to find her before he can herd her back home."

Adam's lips curved into a slow smile and Amelia felt that quivering deep inside begin. All he said was, "Hi. I missed you."

She felt strangely awkward. Maybe it was being here, on Larsen land. Maybe it was because she was waiting for him to ask her to the Farmers Association dance. What if he didn't ask her? She shoved the negative thoughts away. "Really? But you just saw me last night."

His laugh was low. "Actually, I felt you more than saw you last night."

Junior's barking snapped her out of her momentary mental replay of their latest tryst. She turned, almost grateful for the interruption, wondering why she felt so awkward. "What is it, boy? Did you find Wilhelmina?"

The dog barked and then whirled around and raced around the end of the house.

They walked around the side of the large, Victorian-style farmhouse toward several other buildings and barns that held farm equipment and animals. Amelia suddenly became aware of just how vast an enterprise a large farm like this was. Her own place was a mere stalk in the corn field in comparison.

Junior stood next to the front of one barn and Adam pointed to it. "We keep the horses in that one. And my mother's two cows.

Amelia smiled. "Clementine and Tallulah?"

"Right. Very good."

"Maybe Wilhelmina came to visit them."

"Why not?" he replied. "Let's go look. There's a small pasture behind this barn. That's where they spend most of their days."

They entered through a side door and made their way past the stalls. Amelia couldn't help but notice how much newer and well-maintained this barn was than her own. At the other end they emerged near a pasture about five acres in area. Over by a tree, sharing the cow gossip of the day, they spotted Clementine, Tallulah, and the wandering Wilhelmina.

"I don't know how she managed to get in there," Adam said. "The barn door was shut."

Just then a teenage boy carrying a bucket came out of a shed to their right. "Hi, Mr. Larsen."

"Hi, Pete. Pete, this is Amelia Appleberry. She—"

"Oh, sure," the youth said with a smile, "Miss Appleberry's niece. The one who has power over animals."

Adam and Amelia stared at him. Finally, Adam said, "Where did you hear that?"

Pete shrugged. "At school. Which ended yesterday, I'm happy to say. Anyway, this girl I know, Kelly, said that Miss Appleberry—this Miss Appleberry, not the one who passed away—cured her horse. Thought he was a dog or something. I thought she was making it up, but then this other kid said his little brother's dog was cured, too. I think that's pretty cool. What are you, some kind of animal shrink?"

Amelia laughed, oddly proud of the fact that her helping out some of the animals of Hillview had gotten good reviews at the local high school. "No, not really. I just sort of understand them, I guess."

Adam pointed to the three cows standing in the pasture. "Pete, do you have any idea—"

"Hey," Pete said in surprise, interrupting. "There's three of them. I thought you only had two."

"I do," Adam told him. "The other one is Amelia's. She wandered over here this morning. You don't happen to know how she got in the pasture, do you?"

Pete nodded. "I guess I let her in. Sorry, but I found a cow standing in the yard and thought one of yours had gotten out. So I just opened the barn and in she went. I got busy with some other stuff and didn't notice that there were three of them."

Adam slapped Pete gently on the shoulder. "That's all right. We were just wondering if maybe she'd developed the ability to open doors and gates."

Pete laughed and then looked at them, a frown creasing his brow. "You're kidding, right?"

Amelia giggled and Adam sighed. "Yes, Pete, I was kidding. And I'm glad school's out for you, too. We need the extra help around here."

Pete nodded. "And I need the extra money. I have to save money for a truck I want. And there's college next year. And I'm taking Kelly to the dance and those tickets aren't cheap."

"I feel for you, Pete. Maybe I'll talk to Jason and see if we can get you a raise."

Pete's eyes lit up. "Really? That'd be so cool. Thanks. Well, I guess I'd better be getting back to work. Nice meeting you, Miss Appleberry."

"Nice meeting you, Pete," Amelia replied.

He took a step backward and gave a half salute. "See you at the dance."

To Amelia's surprise, Adam saluted back and said, "We'll be there." Pete hustled off into the barn and Adam turned to Amelia and said, "Oh, my God, I didn't ask if you wanted to go to the banquet." He looked chagrined. "I'm sorry. I guess I just assumed you'd want to go. If you don't want to, don't worry about it. I have to go."

Amelia laughed, partly out of relief. "Don't be silly. I'd love to go."

He kissed her quickly. "So, why don't I help you get Wilhelmina back home? I've got a trailer. Won't take a minute." With that he hurried off. Amelia went to retrieve her errant cow. When Adam returned, they were waiting for him.

"We're all set up," he said, taking Wilhelmina's rope and leading her to the trailer.

Twenty minutes later the cow was back in her own stall in the Appleberry barn and Amelia and Adam sat in her kitchen, having a glass of iced tea.

Adam leaned back in his chair. "So, what've you been doing today?"

Amelia smiled and said, "Oh, Mrs. Kappelman came and got Klaus this afternoon. He seemed to be glad to see her. It's hard to tell with cats sometimes."

"Does it bother you that people keep dropping their animals with weird problems on you?"

Amelia shook her head. "Not at all. I love it. And Mrs. Kappelman even gave me a check for twenty dollars."

"Really?"

Amelia protested. "I can't keep it. I told her I didn't want it, but she said something about valuing my abilities or something."

Adam became more serious. "And so you should. But

is psychoanalyzing neurotic animals something you want to be doing a lot of? Although, I'll admit that I didn't think you'd get anywhere with that goat—"

"Cy," Amelia reminded him.

"Yeah, Cy. And what happened with the barking horse?"

"Horace is back home with Kelly; and he may like dogs now, but he has a pretty good handle on being a horse."

"You may not know what you want to do forever," he acknowledged, "but if all these people gave you twenty bucks, you would be able to buy groceries for a month or so."

Amelia could see that Adam thought it was silly. Maybe it was. Although it wasn't any sillier than some of the other things she'd done. For now she just said, "The only thing I know right now is that I'm no farmer."

He didn't whoop and yell 'I told you so,' and for that, Amelia was grateful. He contemplated her announcement before saying, "Well, it's not for everyone. Although, you have got a pretty good garden there."

"I have, haven't I? But anything bigger than that would overwhelm me," she admitted.

"So, back to the drawing board?"

"I suppose," she said quietly. Adam rose and reached out to draw her to him in a tight hug of reassurance.

"Don't worry. If you don't come up with something, it'll come to you."

Amelia wasn't so sure. "You think?"

"I know," he said confidently. "You're smart and creative and you'll figure it out." Amelia hugged him to her, loving the solid warmth of his body, the strength of his arms as they held her to him. She realized in a blinding flash of intuition that she loved him. But until she was sure how he felt, she couldn't tell him.

Never good at concealing her emotions, Amelia still couldn't tear her gaze from his face as he leaned back to look at her. His eyes narrowed and Amelia was sure he knew. But then he smiled rather wickedly and those eyes closed as his head dipped toward hers for a kiss that went from sweetly reassuring to searingly sexual in seconds flat.

"I know I was here just last night, but I can't get enough of you," he whispered against her lips and cheek. He launched a sensual assault on her ear with his tongue that had her squirming against him, her hands restlessly moving on his chest.

They moved in unison and Amelia thought they were going upstairs to her bed, but then she felt the smoothness of the wall at her back. It became clear to her that Adam had no intention of going anywhere else when he shrugged out of his shirt, then pulled her tee-shirt over her head and tossed it on the floor, along with her bra. A thrill of erotic adventurism zipped through her as he looked at her through heavy-lidded eyes. Then his head bent again and Amelia felt her heartbeat double its rate.

His lips nipped along her throat and across her chest to her breasts. He savored each with the raspy silk of his tongue and teased gently with his teeth until she was twisting against him, eager for him to assuage the ache he created. Finally he sucked one exquisitely sensitive peak into his mouth and Amelia gasped from the intensity of the pleasure.

His hands were almost shaking as he opened the snap

to her shorts and slid the zipper down, reaching inside to stroke her intimately. She arched against his hand as he found her slick warmth. One touch of his fingers and Amelia was clutching at his shoulders and struggling to remain standing as her knees turned to water.

Adam pushed her shorts and lacy bikini panties past her hips and they fell to her ankles. Her own fingers quickly dealt with his jeans and he lifted her against him and she opened her legs and slid them around his waist, cradling him between her thighs. She opened to him and welcomed the hard thrust which joined them, letting her head fall onto his shoulder, where her mouth and tongue traced a trail along his shoulder and neck to his ear.

Her teeth scraped along his earlobe and her nails dug into his shoulders as he pushed deeper into her with each thrust. One arm around her waist for balance, he slid the other between them and caressed her intimately. Her head fell back against the wall as a guttural sound of pure pleasure escaped her.

The rapidly building pressure in her exploded as his fingers continued their sweet torture. As she convulsed around him, his thrusts became quicker and his breathing more labored until he surged against her one last time, holding her tightly against him as his breath wafted hot against her breast.

"You," he rasped against her skin, "are the most incredible woman I have ever known."

It wasn't a declaration of love, but it was satisfying to hear, nonetheless. Besides, despite her feelings, she wasn't sure she could trust the L-word. And when it was used during sex, it tended to be quickly regretted.

She slid down his body and found that with a little help

from Adam she could stand again. She laughed shakily. "Thanks to you, I may soon need a walker."

"You may not believe this, but I really only intended to have a glass of tea when I came in here."

"Maybe I should invite you in for refreshments more often," Amelia responded coyly.

"Any more often and *I'll* need the walker."

As they got back into their clothes, Amelia couldn't believe what she'd just done. She'd never been that uninhibited and, well, wild with a man. It was Adam, she thought, watching him out of the corner of her eye as she pulled her shorts back on. Her feelings for him ran so much deeper and truer than anything she'd ever felt that it almost scared her.

But how did he feel? He liked her, obviously, but did he feel anything more for her? It was probably too soon for him, she knew. Some people knew in an instant, some in a week, some not for months or even years.

"Why are you suddenly so quiet?"

His soft words hung between them. Amelia wasn't ready to talk about her feelings yet, so she shook her head and said, "Lots of things. Like, what should I wear to this farmers' gala thing?"

One eyebrow rose, attesting to his disbelief, but he didn't call her on it. "It's semi-formal, I guess."

They talked about inconsequential things then. And after a few minutes, Adam announced he had to get back.

"They'll be wondering what happened to me. And knowing Joe and Harry, they'll come looking for me."

Amelia walked him out to his truck. He kissed her long and hard and then looked into her eyes. "Don't worry about the career thing, Amelia. Maybe if you step back from it, it'll come to you."

With that he kissed her again quickly and hopped into his truck, heading back to his day of work.

Amelia went back into the house, thinking about what he'd said about her future finding her instead of looking so desperately for it. Maybe he was right.

"Pretty passive way to look at it though, huh, Pee-Wee?"

The piglet didn't care what she said, as long at he got fed. Amelia gave him his bottle at the table again and saw Mrs. Kappelman's check still lying there.

"Value your abilities," she said softly.

Her finger tapped the check rhythmically as she hummed a tuneless song. PeeWee may have thought Amelia looked a bit preoccupied, but he didn't mention it.

By the time the night of the dance rolled around, Adam was ready for a party. He'd had equipment failures to deal with all week and one of his hands was sick and the weather had been rainy. Normally that was good. Crops needed rain. But too much rain was as bad as not enough. But the weather forecast was for more rain over the weekend, and most of the people in town were worried. The whole town needed this party, and Adam, for one, wanted to enjoy himself.

"Well, well, big brother," Jason droned from the hallway, "you don't look half as ugly as usual."

Adam dipped his head modestly. "Thank you. Astonishing good looks run in the family."

Jason bowed mockingly in return. "Thank you."

Both brothers wore suits, Adam's dark blue and Jason's a charcoal gray. Adam finished combing his hair and turned to face his brother again.

"Suits, shined shoes, combed hair. We look like a couple of city slickers."

"Speak for yourself, hayseed," Jason said. "I am an example of sardonic splendor whether here or in any metropolis worldwide."

Adam rolled his eyes. "Right."

They headed downstairs where Jason stopped with his hand on the door. "So, you and the Appleberry heir, huh? What's all this about you spending your nights over there?"

Adam shook his head. "One of these days I'm going to move into the jungles of Borneo for some privacy."

"No, you won't. But really, this was pretty fast moving, especially for you."

"What's that supposed to mean?"

Jason shrugged. "Well, you're usually the one who wants to get to know a woman and spend a lot of time with her before you sleep with her. But with Amelia Appleberry . . ."

Adam didn't like the tone of the conversation. Jason was making his relationship with Amelia sound smutty, which it was not. He wasn't exactly sure what it was, but it was not, in any way, smutty. "Watch it, brother," he warned. "I don't think you want to go there."

Jason's eyebrows shot up. "Really? So you're not romancing her for her land?"

Adam knew he probably deserved that, but it annoyed him nevertheless. "I wouldn't do that, and you know it."

"Do I? Does she? I know that you want her land and that it's been a goal of yours for a long time to have it."

How had everything become so frustratingly complicated in such a short time? "Yes, I want the land, but I like to think that I'm above lying to get it."

Jason nodded. "Well, she can't say she didn't know that you wanted her land. You've only offered to buy it a half-dozen times."

"Exactly," Adam said. "Besides, I think that she might be selling it to me after all."

That got Jason's eyebrows even higher. "Really? Why?"

"Because she came here to think about what she wants to do with her future and she decided to try farming."

Jason hooted his amusement at that announcement. "Farming? Did she have any clue as to what that even means?"

"No, but to her credit, she decided to try a garden first. Overworked herself the first day, but didn't give up."

The admiration he had for her tenacity must have shown more than he thought. Jason hummed under his breath and said, "So, she's independent and determined. How do you know she doesn't want to be a farmer?"

"She told me so this afternoon. She said the garden was all she could handle."

"What's she plan to do now?"

That was what Adam wanted to know. "She didn't say. I don't know that she knows."

"But you think she'll sell you the land?"

Adam frowned. "Why shouldn't she? If she isn't going to use it and I'm willing to pay her enough so that she could get a nice house in town."

"Oh," Jason pounced. "So, you're thinking she'll stay in Hillview after giving you her land?"

Adam scowled at his brother. "I think that I should never have told you any of this."

"I'm your brother, not to mention your lawyer; you have to tell me everything. So, if you think she's going to sell you the land, why aren't you happy about it?"

"I only said that, logically, since she's decided not to stay and farm the land, that selling is obviously her best option."

Jason nodded. "Logically?"

Amelia Appleberry. Logic. Adam groaned and rubbed his temples. "You're right. I'm just as much in the dark as I was the day she arrived in Hillview."

The only difference was a huge one. He cared about Amelia and didn't want her leave. But he didn't want her to stay on the Appleberry place. Why couldn't she just sell him the land and move to town? Then he could continue to see her, incorporate the twenty acres into his own, and everyone would be happy.

He just wished he hadn't gotten used to seeing her there. It was almost as if she belonged there.

"Come on, Adam," Jason said, sighing loudly. "You're not going to figure it all out standing here. Maybe you can talk some sense into her at the party."

Adam gave him a look of disgust before walking resignedly out to his truck. Jason shut the door and followed. "Or not."

NINE

The Farmers Association of Hillview County held its annual Banquet and Dance Party at the recently built Hillview Civic Center.

It seemed that everyone who lived in Hillview County was in attendance as Amelia slid out of Adam's truck. It was driven off by a teenage valet, who was quite busy, judging from the long line of vehicles behind them.

If the collection of glittering dresses and smart suits were anything to go by, then this event was one of the biggest of year for the Hillview community.

"Hey there!"

Ned and Nan Winslow hailed them in the lobby. Nan wore a simple blue dress shot through with silvery thread. It swirled around her ankles as she spoke animatedly about the gathering.

"Ain't this the berries? I love these things. Get a chance to get all dressed up and go out dancing."

Ned tugged at the collar of his shirt. "I hope you find a good dance partner. I'm just here for the food."

They all laughed and Amelia said, "I didn't know what a big deal this was. I mean, I knew that people were talking about it, but it looks like everybody who lives in the county is here."

"And then some," Ned agreed.

"You sure look pretty," Nan told Amelia. "Where'd you get that dress?"

Amelia glanced down at the green dress with the hand-kerchief hemline. It floated over her skin, its scooped neckline and fitted bodice giving way to the layers of frothy material ranging from moss to forest green.

"Thank you. I got this in Chicago a couple of years ago. It's the only dressy dress I have."

They moved along with the crowd of people into the banquet hall, where they presented their tickets and were given table assignments. The ticket-taker, a middle-aged woman with a harried expression, greeted Adam with a smile.

"Well, hello, Mr. President. Expected to see you here sooner."

Adam frowned. "Hi, Alice. Why? Isn't everything going all right? Where's Joan?"

"Joan is back in the kitchen arguing with the caterers, last I heard. But that isn't the real problem."

Ned and Nan waved good-bye and wandered off to find their table. People with tickets behind them were being diverted to another ticket-taker.

"And that problem would be?" Adam asked.

"Ed Miller and Ike Shaw got put at the same table."

There was a pause, and from the knowing look that Alice bestowed on Adam and the way that he then sighed and nodded, Amelia figured there must be quite a story behind it.

"I'll take care of it," he said, as he grasped Amelia's elbow and aimed them toward the other end of the hall.

There were dozens of tables, each with a number

placed prominently in the middle. After a few minutes they stopped at the front, center table. It had the number one in its center.

"I'm sorry," Adam said, "but I have to go resolve something. I'll be right back."

Then he was gone and Amelia stared after his retreating back as he weaved through the tables. He finally stopped at one near the center and began talking to a man in a western-style suit, who shook his head a lot and pointed a finger at another man, who suddenly stood up and said something that was swallowed up by the sound of the crowd.

"Nothing like small-town politics, is there, dearie?"

Amelia turned to see Mrs. Kappelman on the other side of her. "Mrs. Kappelman, how nice to see you again. And you look just lovely."

The elderly woman wore an ice-blue beaded gown that looked like it cost a fortune. Her blue eyes twinkled merrily as she said, "I do, don't I?" She reached out and snagged the blue-suited arm of a man standing near her. He turned, an inquisitive look in his eyes.

"Sweetheart, this is Amelia Appleberry. You remember, that nice young lady I told you about who helped Klaus with his problem." To Amelia she said, "This is my husband, Albert Kappelman."

Amelia smiled, remembering Mrs. K.'s story about meeting her schoolteacher love for the first time. "It's so nice to meet you, Mr. Kappelman."

"The same here, young lady. I thought Millie had popped a blood vessel or two when she said she was taking that cat to a shrink, but I was the one who was flabbergasted when the little sneak stopped chasing the bird around the house. How'd you do it?"

Amelia, taken aback by Mr. Kappelman's abrupt praise, struggled for an answer. "Actually, I don't think I can take all the credit. I just explained that it wasn't a nice thing to do and Klaus didn't really believe me, but after a while he came to see my point of view. The sisters helped, of course.

Mr. Kappelman cocked his head. "The sisters? You have sisters out there with you?"

"No, my cats. I named them after the three sisters in the Chekov play."

He nodded. "Right. Olga, Irina, and whatshername."

Amelia fought a bubble of laughter. "Masha."

"Right. Well, whatever you did, it worked. Got tired of rescuing the bird all the time."

Adam reappeared then and they sat down. Mr. and Mrs. Kappelman were also seated at the table. It turned out that Albert Kappelman was also on the city council.

"So what was the drama all about?" Amelia asked.

"Oh, Ed and Ike have hated each other since Moses led them out of the desert. Nobody on the committee noticed they were seated at the same table."

"Why do they hate each other?" She craned her neck, but couldn't see past the two tables behind her.

"Who knows? I don't even know if *they* still know."

"I know."

They both turned to look at Annie Kappelman. She smiled at their curious expressions. "Well, I do."

Adam shook his head. "I'm not sure I want to know."

Amelia wasn't as fatalistic. "I do. What's the story, Mrs. K.?

Millie leaned forward and her husband rolled his eyes. "Here she goes."

"Hush, Albert. Now, not that many know this, because it happened so long ago," she said. "Ed and Ike were both in love with the same woman."

Amelia loved a romantic story. "Really? What happened?"

Millie's expression became rueful. "Well, nothing much really. She didn't pick either of them and they each blamed the other for their loss."

"Oh." As a story of romance, it wasn't the best. "And they're still upset about it? When did this happen?"

She pursed her lips as she thought. "I'd say around 1947 or '48 maybe."

"Fifty years ago?" Adam wished he couldn't believe it, but he'd known Ed and Ike his whole life and he believed it.

"Who was the woman?"

Millie's eyes twinkled again as she leaned toward Amelia. "None other than Grace Appleberry!"

Amelia felt her mouth drop open. "No! Really? Aunt Gracie?"

"Sure. She had most of the men in the county wrapped around her little finger. But she was never serious about any of them. Somebody once said that she must have had a tragic romance of her own because she never married, despite all the offers she got here in Hillview."

Amelia sat back in her chair with a sigh. "I guess I didn't know Aunt Gracie as well as I thought I did."

A bump on the other side of her chair turned her attention to her left. Standing between her and Adam was a man with dark blond hair and laughing blue eyes who had to be related to Adam.

"Well, well, the mystery Appleberry woman revealed at last."

Amelia might have been offended by the words had they not been uttered so charmingly. "That's right. And you must be the equally mysterious barrister brother, Jason Larsen."

As Jason threw back his head and laughed, Adam closed his eyes and said, "Amelia, my brother, Jason."

"Now I know why he's been hiding you," Jason said. "He was afraid I'd make a play for you myself."

"Funny, I don't feel like I've been hiding," Amelia retorted.

"Of course you don't," Jason said, "because Adam is a diabolical sociopath."

She blinked in mock horror. "But he seems so nice."

"That's where the diabolical part comes in."

"If I give you a quarter, will you go away?" Adam demanded merrily.

"My price has gone up," Jason tensed. Then he turned his head to look over his shoulder. "However, you're in luck because my date is getting impatient for my return."

"Who're you with?" Adam asked. "Heather?"

Jason shook his head. "No. Mindy."

Adam shook his head. Jason scowled and waved off his brother's noncomment as he backed away. "See you two later. And, Amelia, don't forget to save me a dance!"

"I won't forget," she promised, then leveled her gaze at Adam. "Why haven't you talked about your brother much? He's charming and funny."

One corner of Adam's mouth quirked upward. "Because he's charming and funny."

"A family characteristic?" Amelia quipped.

"I suppose," Adam acknowledged with a smirk.

"I wonder why he's not here with Heather," she pondered out loud.

"How do you know about Jason and Heather?"

Amelia lifted one shoulder. "I listen around."

Adam sighed.

The waitstaff appeared then and began taking orders. Amelia was surprised to discover that Adam had ordered a special vegetarian meal for her. He shrugged off her thanks. "You have to eat, don't you?"

Besides the Kappelmans, there were two other couples at their table: the Mayor and Mrs. Barker; and the vice president of the Hillview Farmers Association, Roy Kramer, and his wife Polly.

Mrs. Kappelman started a rousing discussion by telling the others about Amelia's amazing ability with animals. Amelia tried to shift the conversation to other topics, but was overridden several times. By the time dessert arrived, she felt embarrassed by the attention, but energized by the possibility of the answer to a prayer.

With dessert also came the speeches from various members of the Farmers Association and local VIPs. Amelia barely heard them. Even Adam's speech about coming together as a community of more than just farmers but neighbors and friends failed to garner her complete attention.

As Mrs. Kappelman and Mrs. Kramer chatted about wayward pets they and their friends had, Amelia slowly chewed her mousse cake and wondered if maybe she hadn't ignored the obvious in her quest for her future.

Dessert over, she fidgeted in her seat as the crowd applauded the speakers and the band began warming up. Adam made his way back to the table slowly, stopping to talk to several people who shook his hand or slapped him on the back in gestures of congratulations.

He barely made it back to the table and Amelia jumped up, unable to sit any longer. "Let's dance," she said, and pulled him onto the already-crowded dance floor.

"What's the hurry?" he protested.

She stopped long enough for him to get his bearings and then stepped into his arms on the beat of the music. The feel of his strong arms around her, the brush of his hips against hers caused her to momentarily forget herself.

She leaned into him, one hand in his, the other on his shoulder. "You're a good dancer," she murmured.

"You don't have to sound surprised," he said with a chuckle. "We have social skills out here in rural America, too, you know."

"I didn't mean it that way," she began, then leaned back to look at him and saw the teasing glint in his blue eyes. She hit him gently. "You know what I meant."

"I know. You feel just right in my arms."

Amelia laughed. "I'm not too soft or too hard?"

He executed a turn to avoid another couple. "No. So, are you enjoying yourself? Mrs. Kappelman seems to think you're the best thing to come along since sliced bread."

Amelia's distraction faded as she remembered why she'd wanted to be alone with Adam. "Right. I'm sorry about that. I didn't intend to monopolize the dinner conversation."

He brushed off her concerns. "Don't worry about it. And you didn't. They wanted to talk to you about what you do with animals; and frankly, it was more interesting than most of the drivel we have to listen to during these dinners."

Amelia preened, eager to share her thoughts with him. "Good, because I've been thinking about something all week. Ever since Mrs. Kappelman came by to get her cat. You know that I've never known what I wanted to do and that this summer was supposed to help me figure that out."

The song ended and everyone applauded, but few left the dance floor. Most stayed as the band struck up the next song, a popular country song that had the crowd forming dance lines. Adam grasped her hand. "Come on. Let's go somewhere where we can hear each other."

He led her to the opposite side of the room where huge glass doors led to a garden. Several people were already there, talking in muted tones. Adam kept Amelia's hand in his as he found a path that wound among apple trees and flowering shrubs.

"Okay," he prompted. "You said that you'd come to some sort of decision?"

Amelia hesitated, not sure if she'd be able to articulate her ideas. "It's so simple, really. I don't know why I didn't think of it before."

He stopped walking and turned to her. "Think of what? You said that day that you knew you didn't want to be a farmer."

"Yes, that's true," she admitted ruefully. "And being

around all these real farmers tonight and hearing about all the things you have to deal with on a daily basis just confirmed it. If I manage to keep my garden thriving, I'll be happy."

"So, if you aren't going to farm the Appleberry Farm—" He left the question hanging between them.

Amelia took a deep breath. "I'm going to devote my time to animal behavior."

Adam nodded slowly. "Okay. But don't you do that now?"

"Well, yes, in a way. But I mean full time. See if I can make a career out of it. So many people have brought me their animals and have been happy with the results. Maybe this is what I was meant to do!"

His expression remained oddly frozen and Amelia felt her enthusiasm slip. Why wasn't he happy for her? Finally he said, "I guess that means you're going to stay on at the Appleberry place?"

She nodded jerkily. He seemed almost angry, and his jaw was clenched. "Adam? What's wrong? Don't you think it's a good idea?"

Finally he said, "I don't suppose you could ever find anything you're more suited to."

Why did that not sound like an enthusiastic endorsement to her?

"That's what I thought," she said. "But you don't seem to like the idea. Why not?"

"Because," he said sharply, then stopped. Then he said, "You know, Amelia, you have to do what's best for you. And if training animals is what you want to do, then why not give it a shot? You've tried everything else."

The abruptness of his answer stung her into silence.

She'd expected him to be glad for her, but instead, he seemed disappointed and even angry. She hadn't expected him to throw her past failures in her face, and she felt tears spring to her eyes. She tried to blink them away before he could see that he'd hurt her, and was grateful when a passing couple chose that moment to stop and talk with him.

They ended up walking back to the banquet hall with them as the two men discussed some problems that had come up recently with government contracts. Amelia, unable to follow half of what they said, walked along quietly, her mind churning.

She tried going over what had happened, but couldn't come up with a reason for Adam's abrupt mood change. He'd seemed so happy, teasing her and laughing. But now . . . now she just felt confused and hurt. And growing a little angry herself. She finally had good news about her life, and the one person she wanted to share it with appeared to hate it.

They made it back to their table just in time for Adam to be waylaid yet again, this time by the mayor. "I'm sorry," he told her, "I'll be right back."

"That's all right," Amelia assured him.

He disappeared into the crowd then. Amelia started to sit down, but felt a tap on her shoulder. She turned to find Jason Larsen beside her.

"Hello, there, where'd you and my brother get off to?"

Amelia smiled as best she could. "We just went for short walk in the garden. It's lovely out there."

Jason hummed something that might have been agreement. "I want to claim my dance. He can't have all of them."

Amelia didn't feel like dancing anymore, but neither did she want to be rude. "I don't think he wants them all."

"I think he does," Jason said cryptically before capturing her hand and practically dragging her toward the dance floor. At least the band was no longer playing line dancing music. "So," Jason said as he swung her into his arms with practiced ease, "how do you like our little town soiree?"

Amelia wasn't sure if he were joking or not. "I like it," she said. "Hillview puts on just as sophisticated a soiree as Milwaukee or Chicago. Its just that you actually know most of the people here. And I do mean you. I only know some of them."

Jason's laugh sounded genuine this time. "Yes, well, you've only been in town a few weeks. And yet you've already managed to make quite an impression. Do you really have a lizard?"

"She's actually an iguana." Amelia corrected.

"Same difference," he insisted. "And you're apparently a wizard of an animal psychologist."

Amelia almost stumbled. "And who told you that?"

"You're the talk of the town. But mostly from what Adam's told me. Occasionally we actually see each other as we pass through the house."

"And he told you I was an animal psychologist?" She doubted it. It wasn't a phrase Adam would use. Amelia might, but that was different.

Jason shook his blond head. "No, he just said you had a bunch of weird animals and that you'd started to take in other people's problem animals to break them of bad habits. Which is what human psychologists do. Any success?"

"As a matter of fact, yes."

"Good for you." He paused as he took her through a complicated turn. Then, "So, Adam said that you'd decided not to be a farmer."

"Well," she said, gazing at him in surprise, "you two just talk about everything, don't you?"

"Not even close," he contradicted. "But we are brothers."

"And he told you about my farming . . . experiment?"

Jason nodded solemnly, but a smile lurked behind that facade. "He did. He also told me that despite beginning in total ignorance, you've managed to cultivate a nice little patch of vegetables."

That surprised her. "Really? I guess that's a pretty apt description. But, my modest success aside, I realized I'm no farmer."

"So he said. He's been torn about your sallying forth into his territory, you know."

Amelia didn't know how to take that. "What do you mean?"

"Well, you know that he's wanted the Appleberry land for a while now and when your aunt passed away, he thought he could buy it from you, but you didn't want to sell. Then you showed up here to live on the place and he saw his plans going up in smoke. But now that you've given up farming, I suppose you'll sell him the land so I can get some peace."

He sounded serious, but Amelia couldn't read him. He was worse than Adam. "Twenty acres," she mused.

"Hmm?"

"It's so absurd that twenty acres of land could mean so much."

Jason looked out over the crowd. "Adam usually gets what he wants. He never understood why your aunt wouldn't sell, and he expected you to sell when he asked you. When you didn't, he had to rethink everything. And it wasn't easy. He doesn't adapt too well that way. But now you've decided to sell and everything's the way it should be."

"Is it?"

Amelia's head was swimming with contradictions. Adam had told her all along that he wanted to buy her land, but had she not realized just how badly he wanted it? Was that why he'd suddenly lashed out at her, out of frustration because she wasn't following his plan? Had he been manipulating her all along? Had all his attention been a means to an end? Had his lovemaking been—

"Is what?"

She looked up into Jason's confused face. "Is what what?"

His frown deepened. "Now I see what he means," he muttered. "You said 'is it?' and I said 'is what?' Maybe I should've said 'is it what?' "

Now Amelia frowned up at Jason. "What are you talking about?"

"I don't know. You started it."

Amelia's mind was going too fast for her feet to keep up and she stopped dancing so abruptly Jason bumped into her.

"Amelia? Is something wrong?"

"I'm sorry. I have to do something." And with that she turned and hurried away. She had to get away to think.

She heard Jason call her name, but she didn't stop. She didn't know where she was going as she made her way through the crowd.

A hand grasp her upper arm and she spun around to find Adam looking down at her. "Amelia? Where are you going?"

"I'm not going anywhere, Adam. But I am leaving," she said, more calmly than she thought possible. She pulled her arm away and watched as his eyes narrowed.

"What do you mean? You seem upset."

That was something she couldn't control, she thought. "Maybe that's because I *am* upset. Tell me something . . . Did you think that you'd get me to sell you my inheritance by sleeping with me?"

He flinched and responded hotly, "No, I didn't."

She went on, "I have to give you credit for one thing. You never lied about wanting my land. You were up front about that. When the straightforward approach didn't work, did you decide to seduce me in the hope that I'd sell it to my lover if not my neighbor?"

A nerve ticked at his jawline as he ground his teeth. "No, I didn't. I told you that I'd never—"

"Yes," she interrupted. "I know that you said it, but did you mean it? Maybe I should've waited longer; maybe I was just too blind to see what you were doing. And I thought you'd be happy that I'd found something to do with my life."

She started to turn, but his words stopped her. "You mean playing animal shrink? Come on, Amelia. Do you really believe that? Isn't this just the latest in a long line of career choices? What's going to happen when you run out of money? Do you really think there are enough crazy animals around here to pay the taxes on that little farm?"

Amelia mustered the last shreds of her dignity and tilted her chin defiantly as she looked at him. "Whatever happens to me financially, they'll be making snowballs in hell before I sell out to you."

Energized by her outburst, she walked quickly away, determined to make it home before she burst into the tears that threatened to choke her.

"Hey there, Miss Amelia, having fun?"

She looked through slightly blurry eyes at Joe, the ever-present Harry at his elbow. They grinned at her.

"Actually, Joe," she said stiffly, "I'm having a perfectly lousy time."

Harry looked at Joe and Joe looked at Harry and both of them looked uncomfortable. Harry said, "Well, uh, is there anything we can do?"

Amelia grasped at the proffered lifeline. "Yes, you can. You can take me home."

The two look at each other again. "Uh, what about Mr. Adam? Why don't you ask him?" Joe inquired.

"I will *walk* back before I let that happen." She saw them exchange another look and took a deep breath. "Look, guys, I know he's your boss; and if you don't want to help me out of loyalty to him, I understand. I'm sure I can get a ride from someone else.

They both bristled. Joe stabbed the air with a finger. "Just because we work for him don't mean we don't live our own lives. Ain't that right, Harry?"

"Damn straight," Harry agreed. "Besides, I don't think he'd really mind, do you?"

Amelia gritted her teeth. "Probably not. Now, can we just go? I really don't want to be here anymore."

It only took them a few minutes to make their way outside and, since no one else had left yet, an even shorter time to retrieve Joe's dilapidated truck from the amused valet. Amelia sat next to the window, her arms folded under her breasts, pressed against her stomach. She didn't care if the dirt from the truck got on her best dress and she didn't dare look back.

Adam made it to the door just in time to see Joe's truck pull away. He glimpsed Amelia's tense silhouette and slapped his thigh.

"Damn!"

Jason opened the door and poked his head out. "What's going on? You almost knocked Old Lady Haber down."

Adam didn't know what was going on, just that everything he was building in his life had disintegrated in one evening.

"Amelia just left," he said, his eyes still watching the driveway but his mind trying to figure out what his next step should be.

"Oh," Jason said quietly. "I thought she seemed sort of . . . distracted earlier. What's wrong? Did she decide not to sell after all?"

It took Adam a minute for his brother's words to sink in, then he turned and pinned Jason with a glare. "What do you mean, did she decide not to sell? She never said she would sell."

Jason looked surprised. "I thought you said earlier that she'd decided not to farm."

"That didn't mean she agreed to sell," Adam pointed

out. "And why did you bring this up, anyway? Did you talk to her tonight?"

Jason suddenly looked guilty and Adam groaned. "We were dancing and I said something about her selling and she said something about twenty acres meaning so much and then I said something about it meaning a lot to you and then she got weird."

Adam practically pounced on him. "Weird? What the hell does that mean?"

"It means she started saying things that didn't make sense. Now, as a lawyer, I'm used to a certain degree of double-talk, but Amelia had me going in circles."

"What did she say?" Adam bit out.

"I just told you. Then she left. I don't know where she went."

Adam knew. She'd found him and he'd opened his big mouth and . . . and now she'd taken off. "I have to go," he said absently.

Jason's eyes widened. "No, you can't. You're the president of the association."

"Well, too bad. I have to go talk to Amelia."

"What if she doesn't want to talk to you?"

Adam shouted to the valet to get his truck, then turned back to Jason. "Then she'll have to listen while I talk."

In the distance, a clap of thunder captured both brothers' attention. The moon was obscured by thick clouds and the air smelled of rain. Adam wondered why he hadn't noticed it when he first came outside. Too preoccupied with Amelia, he thought.

"Supposed to be thunderstorms later tonight and tomorrow," Jason said, watching the sky.

The valet arrived with Adam's truck, and as he headed

toward it, he said, "I wouldn't be at all surprised if I got washed away in a flash flood."

He slammed the door after getting in the truck and sped off. Jason stood under the canopy with the valet and muttered, "What the hell did that mean?"

TEN

Adam swore the whole way to the Appleberry place. Mostly, the derogatory comments were aimed at himself. He cussed himself for what he'd said to her. He cussed himself for leaving the party. He cussed himself for letting love of the land get in the way of his new relationship with Amelia.

But most of all he cussed himself for being stupid enough to fall in love with a woman he barely knew. He tried to think logically and told himself it was probably just lust or infatuation, but he couldn't make himself believe it. He'd known Amelia was the woman he'd been waiting for from the moment he'd kissed her.

And now he'd blown it.

The sky was pitch-black with thunderclouds that covered the moon. He turned onto Appleberry land without a clue as to what he would say to her. Of course, he could apologize, but after that, what?

Adam spied Harry's truck leaving as he pulled to a stop in front of the house. He saw Harry's scrawny arm waving from his open window and pulled to a stop beside him.

"I don't think she wants to talk to you right now, boss," Harry informed him.

"Too bad," Adam replied. "I want to talk to her."

Joe leaned across Harry. "Storm brewing."

"I know that," Adam snapped. "Why don't you two go over and check to make sure we're ready in case it's a bad one?"

Harry and Joe looked at each other in surprise. "Okay," Joe said.

"Will do," Harry assured him. Then he looked over at the house. The only light was the muted glow from her upstairs bedroom window. "I'd still leave her be for a while, Mr. Adam. She ain't whatcha'd call in a talkative mood."

"Yeah," Joe put in. "She didn't say three words to us all the way over here."

Adam propped his elbow on the door of his truck, rubbing his temple with his fingers. "Well, she doesn't have to talk, but she can listen while I talk."

Harry looked at Joe again, then back at Adam. "Uh, okay. We'll see you . . . uh, later, I guess."

They drove away and Adam realized he'd hit a new low. Now Joe and Harry thought he was nuts. He got out of the truck and walked steadily up to the steps and onto the porch. As he raised his hand to knock, he thought how right Joe and Harry were. He was nuts.

But still, he knocked.

"I should be tending to my own place," he muttered to himself, then knocked again. "Not out here when it's about to rain buckets on me and my—"

His what? He'd almost said girlfriend, but that sounded wrong. But they hadn't had time to develop a more solid relationship. And that was something Adam was determined to remedy.

When she still hadn't answered the door after his third

knock, Adam stepped back onto the front lawn and looked up at her bedroom window.

"I know you're in there, Amelia!" he yelled up at her. He could see her silhouette moving from one side of the room to the other. Pacing.

"Amelia, ignoring me won't make me go away! Now come down here and talk to me!"

After a moment, her shadow disappeared and he saw the foyer light come on. A wary sense of relief flooded through him. It was hardly a victory, but at least she was willing to talk.

The front door flung open as the porch light came on to reveal Amelia still in her party dress, her body rigid, revealing an as-yet-unseen facet of the soft, sweet woman he'd fallen for. Adam's shaky confidence almost evaporated.

"Adam, just go away and leave me alone."

"No," he replied, more calmly than he thought possible. "We have to talk about this. I'm sorry about what I said earlier."

She gripped the door frame and nodded. "Fine. Is that it?"

An odd squeaking sound came from behind her and she looked down, then bent to pick up something. Probably Fife, Adam thought, then realized that she was holding the piglet, PeeWee.

"He looks pretty good," Adam observed.

Amelia stroked PeeWee's little head. Adam wondered what she was going to do when he was a three-hundred-pound hog.

"He's doing great, according to Doc Harris."

"Amelia," he began, retracing his steps toward the

porch, "I want to talk to you. I didn't mean what I said. I was just . . . I don't know . . . frustrated, I guess."

"That's all right," she said stiffly. "It's in moments of anger and frustration that true feelings are often revealed. I shouldn't have been surprised that you thought it was a stupid idea. But for some reason, I thought that you would be supportive.

"Amelia," he began again, his foot on the bottom step, "can't we—"

"No, we can't," she said slowly. "I should've paid more attention. I should've realized that you wanted the land more than anything. I thought that what we had found together was bigger than something so tangible as land, but I was wrong."

He took another step and said, "No, you weren't. Yes, I want the land. I've always wanted it, but I never meant to hurt you. Can I come in? I think we should talk about this."

In the glare of the porch light, Adam saw a sheen of tears in her dark eyes, and the knowledge that he'd caused her to cry wrenched his gut and doubled his resolve. But Amelia wasn't cooperating.

"I'd rather not. I have a lot of thinking to do and I can't do that with you here."

"But we need to talk this out," he insisted. Didn't she realize that the sooner they hashed it out, the sooner things could be fixed? At least that's what he hoped.

"I think plenty has been said already," she snapped.

"I said I was sorry," he repeated, but he had the feeling that she wasn't in a forgiving mood.

"I know that. But I don't care right now."

A clap of thunder made both of them jump, and Adam

wanted nothing more than to pull her into his arms and hold her throughout the coming storm. But as he looked up into the inky sky, he knew that wasn't possible. Responsibility pulled at him, and though he didn't want to, he backed away from the steps.

"The storm's probably going to be a bad one," he said. "I have to make sure we're ready to withstand it. There's not a lot you can do when Mother Nature hits you, but trying to control the damage before it hits is something we can do. Or at least try. You should close your shutters and make sure the barn is secure and the animals are dry and fed."

A flicker of concern crossed her face and she nodded. "I will." Then she tilted her chin and said defiantly, "You don't have to worry about me. I'm not helpless or stupid."

Adam groaned in frustration. "I never said you were," he began, but Amelia jabbed a finger at him from the other side of the screen.

"You thought it, though."

"Now you're a mind reader?"

Her mouth shut with an audible snap, and she said through clenched teeth, "I will manage just fine. Why don't you take yourself back to your hundreds of acres and get off my piddly little twenty? You may think of it as the completion of your dynasty, but my aunt Gracie wouldn't sell it to you and neither will I. Now get off my property!"

Adam threw up his hands and headed for his truck. "Fine! I'm leaving. Nice to know I was involved with such a thoughtful and forgiving woman."

He yanked the door to his truck open and then slammed it shut behind him. His thoughts were as stormy as the night as he started the truck and threw it into gear. With no care given to his transmission or tires, he stomped on the accelerator and slung gravel several feet behind him as he sped away from Amelia Appleberry and her lousy twenty acres of land.

Amelia watched Adam disappear in a cloud of dust and gravel and tried to hate him, but couldn't. She shut the door and looked down at PeeWee, nestled in the crook of her arm and whispered, "There is nothing fair about love and I'm sure the same goes for war."

Amelia put him back on the floor and smiled tearily as he scampered away. Then the lump in her throat swelled and she sank onto the floor, her back against the closed door, and sobbed.

Why did it always turn out like this? she wondered. No matter how great she thought a guy was, he always ended up hurting her. But she'd really thought Adam Larsen was different.

"Shows how much I know," she choked and sniffled. She started to look in her pocket for a tissue, then realized that her party dress had no pockets. So she wiped at her streaming eyes with the back of her hand.

When she opened her eyes again, she saw Junior and Fife, plus the three sisters, hovering around her. Even PeeWee teetered anxiously near Fife. "Oh, I'm fine, guys, really," she told them, feeling guilty that her emotional state had become noticeable to her menagerie. "I'll get over him in two or three years and everything will be back to normal."

She could tell by their concerned expressions that they didn't believe her. "Well, okay, what fun is normal any-way?"

She cleared her throat and struggled to her feet, sniffing loudly. "Let's go change and then we'll check on the barn critters and batten down the hatches, okay?"

They seemed to agree with her and followed her up the stairs, watching as she changed into a pair of jeans, a lightweight sweatshirt, and a pair of sneakers. Then she made her way back downstairs and out the side door, allowing only Junior to accompany her outside.

The wind had really started to pick up and she could smell the rain hanging heavy above her. Another thunderclap startled her, and Junior whined and pressed himself against her leg. Amelia leaned down and patted his head.

"It's all right, boy. Come on."

They hurried to the barn and quickly checked to make sure the animals were all right and had plenty of water and hay. She looked in on the pigs and found them nestled snugly together under an overhang built to shelter them from the sun and rain.

The chickens, including Rickles, were secure in the coop; and except for some alarmed clucking and an occasional eruption of nervous crowing from the bantam rooster, they were all right. She pulled down a tarp that was secured on top of the coop to cover its sides. Ned had told her that it was for rainy days so the chickens wouldn't get wet. Because, according to him, it wasn't for nothing that the phrase 'madder than a wet hen' had come into being.

It started to rain as Amelia and Junior made their way back to the house. Fat raindrops pelted her, and in the space of a few dozen feet, Amelia was soaked. She and Junior ran the rest of the way, but it didn't help. They were both wet and uncomfortable as they entered the house.

She took an old towel and dried Junior, then squished her way upstairs to change her wet clothes. She toweled her hair dry and braided it quickly. She still had to batten her own hatches—or whatever.

"Shutters," she thought. That's what Adam had said. She didn't like having to follow his advice, but regardless of what had happened between them, he knew storms.

So she ran around to all the windows, opening them and pulling the shutters closed and latching them. Of course, this soaked another set of clothes. This time she waited until she was done before taking them off. Then she took the whole pile and put them in the dryer.

"Okay, guys," she said, attempting a cheerful tone as she addressed her troops, who had followed her closely from room to room. "We're all snug in the house. The storm will stop after a while and everything will be all right. Right?"

They just looked up at her. Fife shook uncontrollably and Amelia took pity on him. "Oh, Fife, you poor little guy. You know what? Let's make cookies and then watch TV. How's that sound?"

It was at that moment that the lights went out. Amelia swallowed thickly and clutched the Chihuahua to her chest as he whined. "Well, on to plan B," she said, trying to reassure herself as much as the animals.

"How about we light some candles and listen to our battery-powered radio for some weather updates?"

The animals didn't seem to care, especially when another thunderclap sent the three sisters flying upstairs. Fife continued to shake and Junior plastered himself to

Amelia's leg. PeeWee trotted up and oinked his tinny oink at her. "Well, at least someone isn't afraid," she said to no one in particular. Then she noticed that the loud sound had scared something resembling fertilizer right out of her new little friend.

"I know how you feel, PeeWee," she sighed.

The storm pelted the house for hours. Amelia sat huddled in her bed with her menagerie around her. Even Kojak and Larry, Curly, and Moe were brought upstairs. Zilla rested under the heat of the lamp, and the soothing music of Erik Satie played softly from Amelia's portable cassette player.

The thunder finally stopped, but then Amelia heard an uneven staccato beating against the roof. Hail.

"It's okay," she told her frightened animals. "It's just Mother Nature letting loose a bit. We're all safe and warm and dry in here, aren't we?"

They all looked at her with trust, but a certain amount of wariness. Amelia couldn't blame them. She had to admit to being a little frightened herself. And it annoyed her that all she could think about was Adam. She missed his patient, encouraging voice, his quick smile, and the way his eyes would get big whenever she suggested something less than ordinary.

She groaned and pulled the covers tighter around her. He wouldn't leave her head. Images of his face, memories of his touch were etched on her mind. And closing her eyes only made it worse. She could see them together, bodies sliding against each other, straining . . .

"Geez," she said aloud, hitting herself on the top of her head. "Cut it out, already."

Junior cocked his head at her quizzically and Fife growled. "You were right all along, Fife," she told the shivering dog.

She couldn't just sit in bed, so she got up and went to the window, listening to the hail beat against the roof. She opened the shutters and looked out into the darkness.

Wind whipped at her hair and she could see small hailstones bouncing off the windowsill, but it was too dark outside to see anything else. Nevertheless, her gaze shifted to the west. The Larsen farm was out there in the darkness, she thought.

"I hope he's all right," she murmured absently.

A hailstone hit her arm and jerked her mind back to her own problems. She pulled the shutters closed and latched them, then shut the window. "How about a nice cup of cocoa? Oh, right," she remembered, "it's an electric stove. Well, then, I vote for going to bed and hoping all this goes away before we wake up. All in favor?"

Junior barked; Fife growled, and PeeWee sort of oinked. Kojak squawked once and the three sisters huddled together in a caucus and Zilla abstained, as usual.

"Vote's over, motion carried. Everybody go to sleep," she announced. She only hoped that she could follow her own edict and actually fall asleep. Her mind was still a jumble of all the things that had happened today and in the last several weeks. Ever since Aunt Gracie had passed away.

Amelia climbed into bed and rearranged the animals to make room for her legs. "Aunt Gracie," she said quietly, "if you're out there listening, I hope that you don't take this personally or anything, but right now I think this place is more trouble than it's worth."

It was quite awhile before she finally drifted off to sleep, and then her dreams were of Adam Larsen.

The ringing of the telephone woke Amelia the next morning. The persistent, albeit strangely disjointed, dreams of Adam were mercifully ended and she struggled to emerge from her cocoon of covers.

"All right," she mumbled, "I'm coming."

She staggered downstairs in her thin summer chemise nightgown to the only phone Aunt Gracie had installed, the one in the living room, and picked up the receiver. "Hello?"

But the line was dead. She replaced the receiver and shook her head. "No one has any patience anymore. It only rang eight or nine times."

Since she was up, she padded to the kitchen and let the dogs and PeeWee out, then checked to see if the power was back on, which it wasn't. "Okay," she told Olga, who jumped up on the counter, only to be placed back on the floor, "I guess we'll have, um, Pop Tarts for breakfast."

Olga preferred her own food and so did her sisters, who came running as soon as Amelia popped the top on the first can of cat food. While they ate, she let in the dogs and wiped their wet feet, as well as PeeWee's tiny hooves. That done, she took her Pop Tart and went to the side door, gazing outside.

"Barn looks pretty good from here," she said, quietly munching her pastry treat. "But looks can be deceiving, can't they?"

An image of Adam popped immediately into her head
and she had to concentrate to get rid of it. When that
didn't work, she jammed her feet into a pair of work boots
next to the door and left the house, headed for the barn.

She was halfway there before she realized she was still
wearing her shorty nightgown. She slowed, then
shrugged. It wasn't as if there were anybody around to
see her. She shivered in the cool morning air, but didn't
mind.

The ground was squishy and muddy where there wasn't
grass and it sucked at her unlaced boots as she trudged
up to the barn. The animals seemed glad to see her, and
greeted her with a symphony of moos, whinnies, and
bleats. "I'm glad to see you, too," she told them.

She fed and watered them, then let them all out of their
stalls to wander into the pasture or around the corral as
they pleased as she checked on PeeWee's siblings, who
were all growing quickly, running around the sty squealing as she dumped food into the trough. "I don't know
what you're so excited about," she said to the piglets.
"You can't reach the trough yet anyway."

From there she made her way back into the barn and
to the side door that led to the chicken coop. Rickles and
the hens were all fine and dry under the tarp. She threw
it back up on top of the coop and let the chickens out into
the muddy yard. Instead of flinging the feed, she placed
it in piles. "Who wants to scrounge in the mud for breakfast?" she asked, and the chickens seemed to like the idea.
Rickles crowed a few times and tried to strut around, but
the mud pulled at his feet, so he went to sulk near the
fence.

Amelia gathered half-a-dozen eggs and opened the

door to the barn and came face to face with Adam. She gasped in fright, and almost dropped the eggs.

"You scared me half to death," she exclaimed.

He seemed agitated. "Amelia, are you all right?"

Sure, she thought, it isn't bad enough that I have to dream about him all night; now he's right here in the flesh. "I'm fine," she said coolly, trying to get her emotional bearings. "How are you?"

He sighed and she wondered what had frustrated him. He sighed like that, long and loudly, when he was frustrated. Maybe it was his version of counting to ten, she mused.

"You didn't answer your phone and I got worried," he replied.

"Was that you?"

He rubbed his unshaven jaw and Amelia noticed that he had dark circles under his eyes and his hair was a mess. "You look awful . . . ly tired," she said, trying to save a gaffe and not succeeding. Adam just waved it off.

"I know. I've been up all night. The storm damaged some of the crops, and we've been working on damage control. I was worried about you . . . and the animals; but when I called, you didn't answer, so I came over."

She drank in the sight of him, and she wanted to take him inside and feed him and give him a neck rub and make his troubles go away. But she couldn't do any of that, or any of the other things she wanted to do with him. She looked down at the eggs she carried cradled in the skirt of her nightgown. Her cheeks flamed as she realized she'd been talking to him in her thin cotton nightgown with the hem in her hands, exposing most of her thighs.

The fact that he'd already seen it all wasn't the point.

She felt awkward with him and hated it. "Um, well, we're all fine, as you can see. Thanks for checking, but you didn't have to."

She walked past him, into the barn, and continued toward the house with as much dignity as she could muster. She had almost made it when she heard his voice behind her.

"Some of our crops took a beating last night. Especially the younger ones. I don't suppose you've checked to see how your garden fared?"

The eggs hit the ground this time as Amelia's hand flew up to her face. "My garden! I didn't even think about it."

She ran as fast as the mud-clumped boots would allow around the end of the house and stumbled to a stop at the sight that greeted her.

The garden was totally devastated. The rain and hail had battered the little plants and even washed away some of them. The whole plot resembled a big mud pile. Amelia couldn't stop the strangled sob that escaped her throat. All the work and all her anticipations. Gone.

She felt Adam's presence behind her before she felt his hands touch her shoulders. As much as she didn't want to admit it, she needed his strength. His voice was reassuring. "I know it probably doesn't mean much now, but things like this rarely ever happen."

Amelia shook her head helplessly. "Just to me?"

He pulled her back to his chest and wrapped his arms around her. "No, not just to you. Many of the farmers in the area suffered damaged crops."

Amelia felt a wave of guilt. Her loss couldn't compare to people whose livelihood was at the mercy of the elements. "I, should've thought of that. Did people lose a lot?"

She felt his head shaking. "No, not really. Most of the crops were grown enough to withstand most storms. Unfortunately, the same couldn't be said for yours. Your plants were too young to survive the rain and a hailstorm. One or the other, maybe, but not both."

Amelia wiped her tears away with her fingers and let her hands fall to rest on his arms. "It's just that I worked so hard," she sniffled.

"I know you did," he said, as he turned her around and hugged her to him. Amelia let her head rest on his wide chest; her hands rested on his trim waist. As he talked, she felt his voice rumbling through his chest. "And you did a great job. If this hadn't happened, you would've been sitting at your vegetable stand in September selling your produce."

She sighed raggedly. "But it did happen. Maybe this is Mother Nature's way of telling me to get back to the city where I belong."

His body stilled for a long moment; then he stepped away from her. Amelia felt a sudden sense of loss far greater than what she'd just experienced looking at her destroyed garden. "If that's what you believe" was all he said.

Reality came crashing back in an instant and she took a step backward herself, wrapping her arms around her waist and quickly discovering that they were a poor substitute for Adam's.

"I don't know what to believe right now," she told him. He gazed steadily at her. "You can believe in me."

She wanted to, so desperately, but she couldn't trust

herself. She'd made too many mistakes where he was concerned. "I don't know that I can," she said, and watched as his eyes narrowed and his stance toughened. Watching his defenses go up in front of her tore at her heart.

"Well, you have to decide what's right for you," he said. Then he took a step backward. "I have to get back to my place. Call me if you . . . need anything."

Then he turned and walked away. Amelia watched him disappear around the end of the house and then heard the truck door shut and the engine turn over. The gravel made a softly crunching sound as he drove off.

Gazing forlornly at the shredded remains of her garden, she couldn't help but think that her heart felt the way the garden looked.

Joe and Harry watched as Adam skidded to a stop in front of the main garage.

"Don't look like his little visit went too good," Harry observed as Adam slammed the truck's door shut and then made his way toward the house, his hands jammed into his pockets and his eyes contemplating the ground.

"Your powers of observation are amazing," Joe retorted. "Of course, it didn't go too good. What we need to do is find out exactly why Miz Amelia over there got ticked off to begin with."

"Why dontcha just go ask her?"

Joe shook his head at Harry's useless remark. "Maybe because she wouldn't tell us?"

"How do you know unless you ask her?"

There was enough logic in that statement that Joe

couldn't repudiate it. "Okay," he conceded, "but if she tells us to get lost, it's your fault."

Harry snorted. "Always manages to be my fault anyhow. Don't know why this time should be any different."

They headed for Harry's truck and climbed in. Joe poked a finger into the air. "Now, don't go asking her right out when we get there. Let me do the talking."

Harry started the truck and aimed it toward the road. "You? Why should you do the talking?"

"Why shouldn't I?" Joe countered.

"Maybe we both should."

"Maybe you should just shut up and drive."

It only took a few minutes before they pulled to a stop in Amelia Appleberry's muddy front yard. Harry honked his horn twice, and then they got out of the truck and ambled up to the porch as Amelia opened the front door.

They could tell she was surprised by the look on her face; but since she was a lady and all, she greeted them warmly. "Well, hello," she said. "How are you two doing today?"

Harry tipped his battered cap. "I guess we're doing fine, aren't we, Joe?" he responded politely.

Joe raised his eyebrows in surprise at Harry, but said to Amelia, "Yep, I'd say we're doing fine. And how're you doing today, Miz Amelia?"

Amelia's face looked strained. "I shouldn't complain. I know that the people around here could've lost a lot in last night's storm. Some of them probably did."

Joe nodded. "It was a good one. Strong I mean, but not real nasty, like some can get."

Harry scratched his jaw thoughtfully and said, "You didn't suffer any damage over here, did you?"

Amelia sighed. "The animals are fine, and so are the buildings. But I'm afraid my garden was a definite casualty."

"That's too bad," Joe sympathized. "Looked to be the makings of a right nice garden, too."

"Thank you, Joe," Amelia said. "I thought so, too. But, I can't do anything about it now. So, what brings you two over here? I'm sure you have a lot of after-storm work to do."

Harry nodded. "You got that right. And actually, we was wondering if you knew why Mr. Adam was so outta sorts. He was kinda snappy all morning; then he left and when he came back he was sorta, you know, down in the dumps. Joe and me got the feeling he had been over here."

Joe looked at Harry and nodded in admiration. "That's right," he told Amelia. "And that's exactly how he looked, down in the dumps."

"Did he?" Amelia asked, her eyes glancing to the west quickly before looking back at the two of them. "Well, I don't know what to tell you. It's kind of personal."

Harry nodded. "We kinda figgered it was, on account a the way you had us take you home last night."

"And on account a the way Mr. Adam came back from seeing you today. Before he left he looked kinda worried. But when he came back he just looked . . . you know . . ."

"Down in the dumps?" she finished. They nodded. Then Harry said, "You look a little in the dumps yourself."

"I guess I am," Amelia admitted. "Nothing has worked out the way I wanted it to when I got here."

Joe looked alarmed. "You ain't gonna sell out and move are you?" Harry elbowed him hard in the ribs.

Amelia blinked in surprise, then shook her head. "I don't know what I'm going to do." Then her dark eyes sparked with determination. "But if your boss sent you over here to see if I'd changed my mind about selling, tell him to forget it. Aunt Gracie didn't sell to him and I won't, either. Why she ever left him anything in her will is beyond me. And I thought his manipulating me was low," she added as an aside.

But Joe and Harry had already started their denials. "Mr. Adam doesn't even know we're here."

"We just came over to see how you were doing."

"We thought we might help."

Amelia held up her hand. "All right, all right. I believe you."

Harry had a few more words of defense for his employer. "You know, Miz Amelia, I don't know exactly what Mr. Adam did to rile you up, but I've known that boy since he was a little kid. There ain't a dishonest bone in his body. Is there, Joe?"

Joe shook his head vigorously. "Nope, not one. He's hardworking and decent."

"Your testimonials aren't necessary," Amelia assured them. "Maybe we just weren't meant to be," she added quietly. A faint sheen of tears in her eyes had Joe and Harry shifting uncomfortably.

"Oh, now," Harry began, "everything'll work out. Just you wait and see if it don't."

Joe agreed, bobbing his head up and down. "Just you wait and see."

Amelia didn't look as if she believed them, but she

smiled weakly anyway. "I don't think so, but thanks for the good thoughts."

Joe and Harry backed away toward the truck then. "Well, we gotta be getting back," Harry said.

"Lotta work to be done," Joe added.

Amelia waved. "Thanks for stopping by. But I'll be fine, really. All I need is a little time."

They waved back at her and climbed into the truck. Harry fired it up and soon they were trundling up the drive to the road, where Harry braked and paused, looking at Joe.

"Now what do we do?"

Joe shrugged. "Beats me. Looks like Mr. Adam put his foot in it as far as that Appleberry land goes."

Harry couldn't argue with that. "Ain't that the truth. He prob'ly tried to romance her and buy her land at the same time.

"Can't be done," Joe said. "Ain't surprised she got all riled at him."

"Nope, me neither."

They looked at each other. Then Joe said, "So, now what do we do?"

Harry shrugged. "Beats me."

Joe looked depressed. "Let's get back. Maybe we can think of something later. You hungry?"

Harry pulled out onto the road. "Don't you ever think about anything but your stomach?"

"What?" Joe spread his arms in a gesture of innocence. "All I said was—"

"I heard what you said. You got no soul, Joe. No romance in you," Harry observed.

"I got as much romance as the next guy," Joe countered.

"Wonder what Grace Appleberry left him in her will," Harry pondered.

"What?"

Harry jerked a thumb back toward the Appleberry place. "Didn't you hear what she said about Grace leaving Mr. Adam something in her will?"

"Right. I didn't know she left him anything," Joe said.

"It's a mystery," Harry declared.

"That's what it is, all right," Joe agreed.

ELEVEN

Adam sat at the kitchen table the next morning staring at his coffee cup.

"You going to drink that or watch it?"

His brother's voice startled him, but all he said was, "Shut up."

Jason poured his own cup of coffee and sat down at the table across from Adam. "Good morning to you, too. What the hell happened around here yesterday, anyway? I got stuck in town playing host for you with the Farmers Association and then—"

"I don't want to talk about the Farmers Association," Adam interrupted.

"Okay. So, what happened after you left? Did you go out and talk to her?"

"A little. She didn't want to talk. Then she threw me off the place."

Jason whistled. "Really? What got her so mad?"

Adam glared at his brother. "Something about selling her land to me. Did you forget that you and she had a conversation about that?"

"Right. Sorry. That's why she stormed off?"

Adam shrugged. He couldn't believe he'd let things get so out of hand so quickly. But for the life of him, he couldn't think of what he could've done to avoid it. Except that stupid remark about her wanting to be an animal psychologist.

"That and the fact that I wasn't exactly supportive of her idea to be an animal shrink."

"Yeah, she told me about that, too. You didn't think it was a good idea?"

"Who am I to tell her what to do with her life?" Adam muttered, not caring that Jason was listening.

"Who what?"

"Nothing," Adam told him. "I just might have lost the best thing that ever happened to me."

Jason cleared his throat and said, "You've only known this woman a short time. Are you sure you're ready to make that kind of statement?"

"Time has nothing to do with it, Jason," Adam snapped. "I mean, time can only make it better; but all the time in the world can't add to what isn't there to begin with. What we already have—had—I don't know, was really . . . right. But it probably doesn't matter anymore anyway. I blew it."

Jason reached over and grasped Adam's arm. "Brother, I have no idea what you just said, but it sounded like you love her. And if you do, you need to go tell *her,* not me."

"She wouldn't believe me," Adam said. "She'd think I was saying it to get her lousy twenty acres of land."

Jason whistled under his breath. "Sounds like you've got a problem."

"Thanks for pointing that out."

"What are you going to do?"

Adam shoved his fingers through his hair and then

grasped the back of his neck. He let his hands fall away and said, "I have no idea."

"Okay, let's look at this logically," Jason said. "She feels the same about you, right?"

Adam closed his eyes. "She did, I think." Why was he doubting so much now? "Yes, she did."

"Okay," Jason continued. "So all you need is to let her know how you feel and give her time to see that you really mean it."

Adam didn't like the sound of that. "How much time?"

Jason shook his head. "I don't know. As much time as it takes."

"That might mean more time than I have. She only came here to find out what she wanted to do with her life. She can't have enough money to live here indefinitely without some income . . ."

His words trailed off as he thought again about what she'd said about wanting to be an animal psychologist, and he regretted anew the way he'd dismissed it. But what if . . .

"Adam, you've got a strange look in your eyes," Jason said warily.

"I think I've got an idea," Adam told him as he got up and headed for the door.

Jason protested, "Hey, wait a minute. Aren't you going to tell me what it is?"

But Adam was already gone.

Ned and Nan's Taxidermy and Cheese Emporium looked less gruesome each time Amelia visited. She figured that a couple hundred visits and she'd be able to walk in the door without flinching.

"Well, howdy neighbor," Nan called to her from behind the counter. She was arranging a display of cheese products. "How'd you like that storm last night?"

"It destroyed my garden," Amelia said sadly. And a storm of a different sort destroyed more than that, she didn't add.

Nan tsked at her. "That's too bad. Really. But you know, if you plant a few things right away, you still might be able to get a few vegetables before the fall frost."

Amelia didn't know if she could go through all that again. "Maybe. But it'd have to be a very small garden."

Ned appeared from the back room then, carrying a stuffed skunk, which he set on the nearest display case when he saw Amelia.

"Well, if it isn't the lovely Miss Appleberry. How'd the storm treat you?"

"It got her garden," Nan informed him.

"Too bad," Ned said, nodding sagely. "Things like that happen every so often, though. Goes with the territory. Say, why'd you take off so fast Saturday night? I didn't even get a chance to dance with you. And let me tell you, I cut a mean rug."

Amelia didn't doubt it for a moment. "I . . . ah . . . um . . ." she stuttered, unsure of what she should tell them.

"You were sick? One of your critters was sick? You have a fear of crowds? Dancing makes you itchy?" He chortled and added, "Pick any old excuse if the truth doesn't come to you right away."

"Okay," Amelia confessed. "I'm sorry I left so quickly,

but I wasn't in the mood for a party. Well, I was when I got there, but then I wasn't anymore."

Nan finished her display and leaned her forearms on the counter. "What'd he say?"

Amelia frowned. "What do you mean?"

"I mean that Adam Larsen must've said something to upset you and that's why you left. Everybody at the party was talking about it."

Amelia's eyes widened. "Everybody? Why? How did they know?"

Ned's laugh was barely sympathetic. "Are you kidding? This town's been fairly atwitter with gossip about you ever since you arrived. Every old biddy with a porch and a rocking chair has been placing bets on when you and Adam Larsen would get hitched."

Amelia stared at him, then looked at Nan. "Please tell me he's kidding."

" 'Fraid not, honey. You can't really blame them, though. I mean, they've known Adam all his life and, to put it politely, he's been pretty persnickety about the girls he goes out with. When you and him started mooning over each other, everybody just naturally—"

"We never mooned over each other," Amelia denied.

Nan just looked at her patiently. "Be that as it may, the people around here naturally talked about the two of you. And that business about you and the animals, well, that just made you the topic of conversation all over the county."

"So when you two had that little spat at the farmers' shindig," Ned added, "well, if it hadn't been for the storm, nobody would've talked about anything else."

She should have felt embarrassed, but after the last

couple of days, Amelia just couldn't concern herself with what the people of Hillview thought about her and Adam. Instead, she smiled as brightly as she could muster. "I'm sure that after a while everyone will find something or someone else to talk about."

Ned barked a laugh. "I wouldn't count on it. So, what happened? Why did you take off? What'd he say to set you off?"

Nan slapped at her husband and missed. "Why don't you be quiet? Isn't there a woodchuck or something back there in need of stuffing?"

"Yeah, yeah, I get it. Girls wanna talk. I'm leaving." He started for the back and then turned, a mischievous twinkle in his eye. "Just remember, she'll tell me later!"

"Get out of here," Nan prodded. When she turned back to Amelia, she was shaking her head. "That man. I won't tell him anything you don't want me to tell him."

"There really isn't that much to tell," Amelia began. "And I didn't come over here to dump all my troubles on your doorstep."

"Nonsense. That's what neighbors are for."

"I was just wondering what you thought about my working with the animals around here."

Nan's eyebrows drew together as she pondered the unexpected question. "Well, from what I've heard, you have a real talent for that kind of thing. Why not make it a business?"

Encouraged by Nan's words, Amelia said, "That's what I thought, but do you think that maybe it wouldn't work here because there aren't enough people?"

"Might be a point," Nan agreed. "But you never know 'til you try. Might be able to supplement your income.

That's what Ned and me are doing with this place. How much money do you need?"

Amelia wasn't sure if Nan meant that as a rhetorical question, but she chose to think of it as such. "I need to find something I can do that will support me and the farm or I'll have to sell it. And I really don't want to do that. Especially not . . . Well, let's just say I don't want to sell," she finished.

Nan's smile widened. "Amelia Appleberry, don't you know that we all know that Adam Larsen wants to buy your land? Heck, everybody knows that. He used to pester your Aunt Gracie about practically every week. Why she didn't just sell it to him and move to town is beyond me. She could've wrung a goodly sum out of that man."

"Maybe she just didn't want to leave," Amelia supposed.

"Maybe. And maybe she was just being stubborn. I take it Adam offered to buy and you turned him down?"

Amelia nodded. "Yes."

"Is that what your fight was about? You not wanting to sell the land?"

"Partly," she conceded. "But it's complicated."

Nan thought that was funny. "Love always is, sweetie. Now, the way I see it, you've just got one thing to decide—which would you rather have: twenty acres of land or Adam Larsen?"

"It's not that easy," Amelia protested.

"Isn't it? If you play your cards right, you can have both," Nan added. "And maybe more."

Amelia didn't pretend to understand that last part, but as she left the rustic little store, she considered Nan's words. Was it really just a choice between Adam and her land? It wasn't. There was more to it. There was trust and respect and her aunt Gracie's legacy. Why didn't anyone understand that?

She walked the short distance to the road and checked for speeding trucks before crossing. She retrieved her mail from the red mailbox and had started past the gate when she stopped abruptly.

There, on the gate leading to her property, a sign was stapled to the top rail of the fence. It read:

AMELIA APPLEBERRY, ANIMAL PSYCHOLOGIST
BEHAVIOR MODIFICATION
FOR PETS AND FARM ANIMALS
REASONABLE RATES

She stared at the hand-lettered sign for a moment, wondering where it had come from. Who had put it there? Could it have been Joe and Harry, she wondered, trying to help? Only it seemed too sophisticated for the two of them. And the only other person . . .

Believe in me.

His words echoed in her head. Had Adam done this? And why? If he wanted her to sell, why would he help her like this?

She touched the sign gently along the side before starting for the house. She walked along, looking at the unused pasture acreage around her. Aunt Gracie's house. Funny how she still thought of it as Aunt Gracie's, and not her own. She stopped a few hundred yards from the house and looked at it all. The house, the barn, the shed, the grass, the mud. It was hers.

But at what cost? Could she live here with Adam so

near and not love him? What if he met someone else and
got married and they were right there, one farm over?

The thought chilled her. She'd never be able to watch
him love someone else. But what if she were right after
all? What if he didn't really love her and had only made
love to her to get this little piece of dirt?

Suddenly, Amelia knew what she had to do. She had
to find out how Adam really felt, and there was only one
way to do that. The risks were enormous, but if he really
had made the sign for her and if . . .

If. If. If.

She hurried to the house and went inside. In the living
room, on the little table under the telephone was the
Hillview phone book. Compared to the Chicago phone
book, Hillview's directory was little more than a pam-
phlet. She found what she was looking for quickly and
dialed the number. She heard a woman's voice answer.

"Jason Larsen, Attorney at Law."

After speaking with Adam's brother and convincing
him that she wasn't kidding, Amelia arranged to meet him
at his office in an hour. She then went upstairs to change,
Junior and Fife hot on her heels, wondering what all the
excitement was about.

"I've never done anything like this, guys," she told
them. "But for once in my life, I'm going to take a real
chance. You think I shouldn't?"

They didn't offer much advice, as usual. PeeWee
squealed from the foot of the stairs and Junior went to
haul him up the same way he hauled Fife. Amelia, dressed

in a soft gauzy skirt and blouse, noticed the three sisters
were watching her from the bed.

"Have you seen the shoes that go with this dress,
girls?"

One of the animals, Amelia wasn't sure which yet, had
taken to hiding her shoes. Not chewing or clawing, just
hiding. She'd been so busy taking care of other people's
animals, she'd probably been neglecting her own.

"I promise I'll pay more attention to you," she told
them. "Now, where are the shoes?"

Junior disappeared at a trot and returned a minute later
with one of the shoes in his mouth. He dropped it at
Amelia's feet and sat down, waving a paw at her.

"Thank you, Junior." She reached down and retrieved
the shoe which the dog had been nice enough not to drool
on. "Now, where's the other?"

Fife growled and then turned and fled through the door
on shaking legs. Amelia didn't see how the little dog
could possibly pick up her shoe, much less fetch it. She
followed him, limping with one shoe on.

"Where are you going? Fife, let Junior get it."

Behind her, Junior and PeeWee barked and oinked. Fife
disappeared behind the door at the top of the stairs.

The attic.

"I thought I closed this door," Amelia murmured.

Junior pushed the door open wide and they all saw Fife
standing with his forefeet on the first step, growling.

"No, Fife, we don't have time to play in the attic. I
have to find—"

But Fife suddenly yodeled a howling sort of bark and
Junior picked him up by his collar and headed up the
stairs.

Amelia sighed and picked up PeeWee, who was danc-ing around at her feet and squealing. She made her way up the narrow stairs to the attic.

It was musty, but otherwise reasonably clean and bright, the two dormer windows letting in cheery patches of sunlight. Moving boxes Amelia had stored shared space with old bird cages, a dressmaker's mannequin, a couple of bedsteads, and other items her aunt Gracie had left.

Amelia beckoned to her wayward pets. "Junior, I don't have much time. Did you put my shoe up here? If not, come on. I have a lot to do today."

Junior responded by putting Fife gently down on the floor and woofing softly. Fife promptly trotted off for the far end of the attic, growling menacingly.

"What is it, Fife? Did you find a mouse? Don't hurt it," Amelia warned.

The little dog disappeared behind one of the solid oak bedsteads and continued his growling.

"Get out of there, Fife. Something could fall and hurt you."

She made her way across the attic and leaned down to pick up Fife, only to find him tugging at the corner of a sheet. "What are you doing?"

Curious, she stepped to the end of the bedstead and saw that the sheet covered up something. She reached into the dark space between the bedstead and the wall and grasped the edge of the sheet and tugged. Fife stumbled backward, still grappling with the offensive sheet. There wasn't much light in this corner, but Amelia could see enough to tell what had been under the sheet. It was a trunk.

"Oh," she breathed, "it must be the trunk Aunt Gracie left to Adam."

Uncaring about the time, she set PeeWee down and shooed the dogs to a safe distance where they were joined by the three sisters, who'd made their way silently up the stairs to join the party.

She carefully moved the bedsteads and leaned them against the adjoining wall. There were a few smaller items—games and such—around it that also had to be moved. Finally, she was able to pull the trunk into the light.

It was just an old black trunk with a curved top and old-fashioned locks. And it didn't seem that it weighed enough to have anything in it. "Now why would Aunt Gracie leave this to Adam?"

The animals had no answers, and neither did she. "Well, I found it. Now what do I do with it?"

Junior barked happily and waved at her. She waved back. "He'll have to wait for his inheritance. I have an appointment to get to. Come on." She then herded everyone downstairs, where she found her other shoe lying under the kitchen table.

As she headed out the front door, she saw Matt O'Brien wheeling up in front of her porch on his bicycle, Leo once again ensconced in the basket.

"Hey, Miss Appleberry."

"Hello, Matt. I'm sorry, but you caught me on my way to town. I have an appointment."

"That's okay," he told her. "I just came by to give you this." He pulled a wadded-up five-dollar bill from his pocket and handed it to her. "I figured I should pay you for helping me with Leo. My mom said you help animals as a job. I wish I could have such a cool job someday. Anyway, she said it would be okay if I gave you my allowance. Leo and me are real glad you helped him."

Amelia wanted to give the little boy his allowance back, but realized that it was important to Matt and probably his mother that she take it. "Well, thank you, Matt. Leo was a good pupil. Weren't you, boy?"

Leo barked and sneezed and Matt laughed along with Amelia. "If there's ever anything you need, just let me know," Matt said, turning his bike around.

Her attention caught by his offer, Amelia stopped short. "Matt, I believe there is something you could do for me," she said. "Do you know Joe and Harry? They work for Mr. Larsen.

Matt nodded. "Sure. They're really old."

Amelia hoped he didn't tell Joe and Harry that. "I'd like you to go over to the Larsen farm and give them a message for me. Could you do that?"

"Sure."

Amelia pulled a piece of scrap paper from her bag and scribbled a note on it, then gave it to Matt. "The only thing is, only give it to Joe or Harry. Nobody else. Okay?"

"No problem," Matt assured her as he crammed the note into his pocket. "Me and Leo can do it."

"I'll be back in about an hour or so," she called to Matt, who was already halfway up the drive. She turned to get into her van, her attention shifting to the meeting she was due at in fifteen minutes. It would either be the best thing in the world or the biggest mistake she'd ever made.

* * *

Matt delivered the note easily enough, since Joe and Harry were sitting on Harry's tailgate in front of the Larsen house when he arrived. Propelled into action by the note, they put Matt and his dog and bike into the back of the truck and drove back over to the Appleberry place, where they went into the unlocked house and made their way to the attic.

Joe found himself surrounded by three cats, two dogs, and a piglet at the bottom of the attic stairs. Harry had gone up ahead of him and turned to look back at Joe. "Are you coming or what?"

"This ratdog won't let go of my pants."

"Get rid of the dog and come on."

Joe disentangled the growling Fife from his pant leg and joined Harry in wrestling the awkward-sized trunk downstairs. Matt yelled instructions to them and kept the curious animals out from underfoot. By the time they'd gotten it into the back of Harry's truck, the two men were breathing heavily and swiping at their faces with hand-kerchiefs.

"Come on, let's go," Matt yelled at them. "I wanna see what's in it!"

Harry waggled a finger at the boy. "I done told you that it ain't none of our business."

Matt looked at the trunk. "But if he opens it while we're still there . . ."

"Then that's different," Joe reasoned. "Now let's get going."

They returned to the Larsens and put the trunk on the front porch. Matt, severely disappointed that Adam wasn't home, took his dog and left. Joe and Harry decided to hang around for a while.

"Whaddya think's in that thing?"

"I don't know, but it couldn't be much. Doesn't weigh enough."

"That's a fact. Couldn't be money."

"Grace Appleberry wasn't a rich woman."

"What would she want to leave to Adam Larsen?"

"Don't know. Have to wait and find out."

"Yep."

Adam had spent the morning working on the irrigation system with several farmhands. And it wasn't going well. His concentration left something to be desired and he'd been worried about how Amelia would feel about the sign he'd put out before going to work. Would she understand what he'd meant or would she still think he was trying to manipulate her?

"Okay," he yelled to one of the hands. "Try it now!"

The man turned a valve that released the flow of water into the divergent pipes, and the joint in front of Adam erupted, spewing water over him and causing two other men to scramble backward, yelling for the first man to turn it off.

"We need a new fitting," Adam snapped, pointing at the offending piece of metal. "The threads on this are so shot that there's no way it'll hold. Wes, didn't I tell you to get some new ones?"

Wes nodded and said, "Yeah, but they haven't come in yet."

"Well, go get on the phone to Jack at the distributor's and find out where the hell they are. We do enough business with them that they should try harder to get our orders in."

Wes gave him a wary look, then took off for the truck. Adam looked up from the offensive pipe to find the other men eyeing him strangely. "What?"

"Nothing," one of them drawled. "We were just wondering what she did."

The other two snickered at that, and Adam said, "She?"

"Yeah, must've been a woman. Never seen you this grouchy before. Woman problems, boss?"

Adam wanted to resent their insight and yell at them some more, but instead he waved them away. "Maybe I'm just hungry. Let's break for lunch."

The men laughed good-naturedly at him as they made their way to the trucks that took them back to the main house. The rest of them headed into town for their favorite cafe. Adam decided to remain home. He wasn't that hungry.

He turned from the drive where he had parked his truck to find Joe and Harry hovering on his porch. "What is it now?"

"Nothing," Harry said, grinning like a fool.

"Nothing at all," Joe added.

It was then that Adam noticed the trunk sitting on the porch between the two men. He knew what it had to be. Still, he asked, "Is that what I think it is?"

Harry nodded. "Yep. Your inheritance from Grace Appleberry.

Adam made no move to open the trunk, or even examine it. "Where'd you get it?"

Joe waved one hand in a generally easterly direction.

"Over at the Appleberry place, where else? Miss Amelia asked us to haul it over here. Don't look like much, does it?"

"And it ain't very heavy, either," Harry told him.

Adam still didn't move. "And what did Amelia say about it?"

Joe and Harry looked at each other, then Harry said, "Nothing. She sent us a note. She wasn't even there when we got it. Just them animals of hers."

"Dang ratdog of hers attacked me," Joe said.

Adam couldn't help but smile at that. Fife the guard dog.

Harry apparently couldn't stand the suspense. "Aintcha gonna open it?"

He didn't really see any way around it. And though he wished Amelia had called him herself about it, he might as well get it over with.

"All right."

He took the few steps to the trunk and leaned over to undo the latches. It wasn't locked. He pulled the lid open and peered inside. Joe and Harry leaned in anxiously as well.

"What is it?"

"I don't know. I can't see. Your big head's in the way."

Adam reached in and picked up the envelope that lay on the bottom of the trunk. "I had a feeling about this," Adam said as he looked at the envelope. "It's probably Miss Grace Appleberry's top ten list to being a better neighbor."

But when he opened the envelope and unfolded the single sheet of paper, he saw that only two lines were written on it in Grace Appleberry's old-fashioned script.

Sometimes the quest for that which you desire most will lead to the discovery of something far more precious.

Joe and Harry read the words over Adam's shoulder. "What the heck does that mean?"

"And what kind of a bequest is it?"

Adam smiled ruefully. "Good old Grace knew exactly what she was doing."

He strode away then, leaving Joe and Harry to ponder his inheritance.

"Sounded like a riddle."

"Think it's a clue to something else?"

"To what?"

"I don't know. Miz Grace sure was different."

"But in a good way."

"That's a fact."

Adam paced in the kitchen, unsure about what to do. His inheritance from Grace Appleberry made perfect sense to him and he wondered if Grace had set him and Amelia up in some cosmic way. Or maybe she had just known how right they were for each other, he thought. Adam kept pacing. He might have lost her. Over what? Twenty acres of land? It seemed almost surreal to him now that just a few weeks ago that land had meant so much to him and now he could only think that it had cost him Amelia.

He reached for the phone to call her, then drew back. No, the telephone was too impersonal. He needed to . . .

An idea formed and he picked up a pencil and piece of paper from the pad next to the phone and started writing.

Amelia returned from her appointment with Jason and discovered that the trunk was gone. Joe and Harry must've taken it over. She wondered if she'd ever find out what was in it.

She went inside and stared at the phone for a while.

Believe in me.

Could she trust him? She loved him; she knew that. But without trust, love couldn't last. That was one of the reasons she'd gone to see Adam's brother.

Jason Larsen had protested loudly when she'd gone to see him. But in the end, he'd gone along with her. It hadn't been all that complicated. But how would Adam react? And why had he put that sign out on the fence? She felt cautiously hopeful. But first, they had to see each other and talk it out. Adam had wanted to talk and she'd reacted by throwing him off her property. She wouldn't blame him if he didn't want to talk to her anymore. But she still had to try.

She reached for the phone, then pulled back. No, she would go over there and see him.

Junior woofed and she turned to see him standing at the side door. "Sorry, Junior. I didn't notice you."

She pulled the door open and Junior trotted out. Naturally, Fife and PeeWee had to follow. Amelia wondered distractedly if PeeWee didn't think that he was really a dog instead of a pig. Well, she'd cured Horace of that notion. PeeWee just needed to spend more time with his brothers and sisters.

She waited impatiently by the door. Now that she had

decided to go see Adam, she wanted to do it before she could talk herself out of it.

While the dogs were out she fed and watered Kojak and the mice; but when she returned to the door, the dogs hadn't come back yet. Impatient to see Adam, she stepped outside to call them. They didn't come, but she heard Junior barking and went to see what he'd discovered.

"Probably a frog," she said to herself.

The barking came from the pasture that took up the whole ten acres behind the house and barn. She walked to the white rail fence and saw Junior barking at a horse that was walking slowly across the pasture. But it wasn't Peaches or Herb. It was Duke. Adam's quarterhorse.

Puzzled, Amelia slipped between the rails of the fence and approached the horse. She looked around, but didn't see anyone. Just Duke, who'd stopped to munch some grass and look balefully at Junior, Fife, and PeeWee, who were creating a cacophony of barks, growls, and oinks.

She hushed the smaller animals. "It's only Duke. How ya doing, fella?"

The horse looked up at her and bobbed his head a few times, but didn't move. Amelia moved close enough to reach out and gently rub the white spot on his head. It was then she noticed that there was a piece of paper tucked under Duke's bridle. Her eyes darted around the pasture again, but she still didn't see Adam. With shaking fingers she took the note and unfolded it.

Lady Animal Psychologist,

Please help me. I'm so sad.
I was a real jerk and may have lost the most beau-

tiful filly in the world. Lately I've been ornery and
mean to the other horses in my paddock. They say
I'm lovesick. I know I am. What should I do?

Amelia's eyes misted over but she ignored them as she
stroked Duke's muzzle and then reached out to hug the
horse. When she let go and stepped back, her eyes swept
the pasture again. Adam was there somewhere, and at last
she glimpsed a jean-covered leg behind a nearby tree. He
didn't say anything, or even move, so Amelia turned back
to Duke.

"You know, Duke, I think that you're being too hard
on yourself. Things like this are rarely one . . . um . . .
horse's fault. It usually takes two people—I mean
horses—to ruin something beautiful." Her voice threatened to fail her, but she swallowed past the lump and
continued. "If you really love your filly, then you should
tell her. Because love between two . . . horses . . . is more
important than anything else."

She could see Adam standing next to the tree, watching
and listening; and she turned to look at him, her eyes still
watery, but her voice strong and clear. "I know that you
can work it out if you really love each other."

"And believe in each other," Adam said as he walked
steadily toward her. Amelia stepped away from Duke and
into Adam's arms. He hugged her with a ferocious tenderness she'd never felt and she knew that everything was
going to be all right.

"I know it's crazy," he murmured against her ear. "I
know that we've only known each other a short time. But
I love you. And I don't care what you do with the land.

Keep it. Use it for an animal mental clinic. If it keeps you near me, I'll be happy."

Amelia laughed through her tears and hugged him to her. "As long as the animals have the barn and room to roam, I don't see why the rest of the land shouldn't be part of Larsen land."

"I'm not asking for your land anymore," he said quickly, pulling back far enough to look at her. "You're here in my arms and that's all I need."

He kissed her fiercely, his lips slanting across hers in a brief kiss of possession and exultation.

"I know you aren't asking," she said, trying to be serious, but the joy in her heart bubbled over and she couldn't stop smiling. Still, she had to tell him. "But it's yours."

He kissed her cheek and her eyelids and the corners of her mouth. "What's mine? You, I hope."

"Yes, definitely me." She laughed. "But also the land. It's no longer the Appleberry place."

He stopped kissing her then and stepped back to look at her. "What are you talking about?"

"I went to see your brother today and legally deeded the property over to you."

He stared at her, then shook his head. "No. Thank you, but that's all right. Keep it."

"I don't want the land," she said. "I just want you. And I don't want it ever to be an issue between us."

"It won't be. Keep it," he insisted.

Duke chose that moment to push against Adam's back, which nudged Adam back into Amelia's arms. She laughed at his surprised expression.

"You aren't using any of that animal psychology on me, are you?"

Amelia wrapped her arms around his neck and kissed him. "No, I just fell in love with you," she whispered, then looked up at him and stroked his jaw. "How about if we hold the land in trust for our firstborn?"

Adam nodded. "I think that's the perfect solution." Amelia thought she saw a sheen of tears in his eyes before they closed and his head bent to hers. This kiss was tender and sweet with the promise of a lifetime together.

They heard barking and growling and oinking and broke apart to look around and laugh. Junior sat there woofing and waving while PeeWee oinked and squealed as he ran a circle around them. Fife bared his teeth and launched himself at Adam's pant leg.

Adam sighed. "I guess the stepdogs will take awhile to accept me."

He leaned over and disentangled the errant guard dog. He straightened and stood with Fife held in the crook of his arm. "Sooner or later, he'll grow to like me," he said. Amelia looked at Adam and smiled happily; then she leaned over and whispered something in Fife's ear. The little dog whined and looked up at Adam. Then his tongue came out and quickly licked the back of Adam's hand.

Adam's eyes widened in surprise; then he gazed steadily at Amelia. "All right. What did you tell him?"

She smiled. "I just told him to quit playing hard to get. Because loving you is the easiest thing in the world to do. I finally found out what I was meant to do with the rest of my life."

COMING IN JUNE FROM
ZEBRA BOUQUET ROMANCES

#49 THE MEN OF SUGAR MOUNTAIN: TWO HEARTS
  by Vivian Leiber
__(0-8217-6623-6, $3.99) Kate left home in search of Mr. Right, and thought she'd found him in the big city. Now, broke and rejected by her blueblood husband, Kate is back home. She's determined to salvage her marriage, with some help from an unexpected ally—Sheriff Matt Skylar. Little does she know, the hunky lawman is planning to make her *his* wife!

#50 THE RIGHT CHOICE by Karen Drogin
__(0-8217-6624-4, $3.99) Carly Wexler is planning her wedding the same way she has planned her life—perfectly, with no loose ends or real passion. Though her heart doesn't leap when she thinks of her fiancé, she's certain this union is for the best. Until she meets sexy Mike Novack, who is everything she's trying to avoid . . . hot, passionate, and forbidden.

#51 LOVE IN BLOOM by Michaila Callan
__(0-8217-6625-2 $3.99) Seventeen years ago, model Eva Channing ran from the glamorous world of New York fashion to small town Texas where she could forget her passionate, doomed affair with photographer Carson Brandt. Today, Eva is content . . . until a magazine piece on former models brings Carson tumbling back into her life . . .

#52 WORTH THE WAIT by Kathryn Attalla
__(0-8217-6626-0, $3.99) Abandoned to foster homes as a child, beautiful Charlie Lawson is steel and velvet on the outside but, on the inside, she's vulnerable and lonely. Even though she longs for romance, Charlie decided never to give anyone the chance to hurt her . . . until sexy, compassionate Damian Westfield makes her believe in love again.

Call toll free **1-888-345-BOOK** to order by phone or use this coupon to order by mail.

Name _____

Address _____

City _____ State _____ Zip _____

Please send me the books I have checked above.

I am enclosing	$_____
Plus postage and handling*	$_____
Sales tax (in NY and TN)	$_____
Total amount enclosed	$_____

*Add $2.50 for the first book and $.50 for each additional book.

Send check or money order (no cash or CODs) to:

Kensington Publishing Corp. Dept. C.O., 850 Third Avenue, New York, NY 10022

Prices and numbers subject to change without notice. Valid only in the U.S.

All books will be available 6/1/00. All orders subject to availability.

Visit our website at **www.kensingtonbooks.com.**

ABOUT THE AUTHOR

Patricia Ellis lives with her family in Michigan. She is currently working on her next Zebra Bouquet romance, *Rodeo Hearts,* which will be published in September 2000. Patricia loves hearing from readers and you may write to her c/o Zebra Books. Please include a self-addressed stamped envelope if you wish a response.

<u>BOOK YOUR PLACE ON OUR WEBSITE</u>
<u>AND MAKE THE</u>
<u>READING CONNECTION!</u>

We've created a customized website just for our very special readers, where you can get the inside scoop on everything that's going on with Zebra, Pinnacle and Kensington books.

When you come online, you'll have the exciting opportunity to:

- View covers of upcoming books

- Read sample chapters

- Learn about our future publishing schedule (listed by publication month *and author*)

- Find out when your favorite authors will be visiting a city near you

- Search for and order backlist books from our online catalog

- Check out author bios and background information

- Send e-mail to your favorite authors

- Meet the Kensington staff online

- Join us in weekly chats with authors, readers and other guests

- Get writing guidelines

- AND MUCH MORE!

Visit our website at
http://www.zebrabooks.com